The Finer Points of Sausage Dogs

The Finer Points of Sausage Dogs

Alexander McCall Smith

W F HOWES LTD

This large print edition published in 2004 by
W F Howes Ltd
Units 6/7, Victoria Mills, Fowke Street
Rothley, Leicester LE7 7PJ

1 3 5 7 9 10 8 6 4 2

First published in the United Kingdom in 2003
by Polygon

A CIP catalogue record for this book is available
from the British Library

ISBN 1 84505 661 2

Typeset by Palimpsest Book Production Limited,
Polmont, Stirlingshire
Printed and bound in Great Britain
by Antony Rowe Ltd, Chippenham, Wilts.

This is for

MATTHEW GUREWITSCH

Contents

Contents

THE FINER POINTS
OF SAUSAGE DOGS

Professor Dr Moritz-Maria Von Igelfeld, author of that great triumph of Germanic scholarship, *Portuguese Irregular Verbs*, had never set foot on American shores. It is true that he had corresponded from time to time with a number of noted American philologists – Professor Giles Reid of Cornell, for example, and Professor Paul Lafouche III of Tulane – and it is also true that they had often pressed him to attend the annual meeting of the American Modern Languages Association, but he had never been in a position to accept. Or so von Igelfeld said: the reality was he had never wanted to go and had inevitably come up with some excuse to turn down the invitations.

'I have absolutely no interest in the New World,' von Igelfeld said dismissively to Professor Dr Dr Florianus Prinzel. 'Is there anything there that we

1

can't find in Germany? Anything at all? Can you name one thing?'

Prinzel thought for a moment. Cowboys? He was a secret admirer of cowboy films but he could never mention this to von Igelfeld, who, as far as he knew, had never watched a film in his life, let alone one featuring cowboys. Prinzel rather liked the idea of America, and would have been delighted to be invited there, preferably to somewhere in the West.

Then, one morning, Prinzel's invitation arrived – and from no less an institution than the ideally situated University of San Antonio. This was a city redolent of cowboys and the Mexican border, and Prinzel immediately telephoned von Igelfeld to tell him the good news.

Von Igelfeld congratulated him warmly, but when he replaced the receiver his expression had hardened. It was quite unacceptable that Prinzel should go to America before he did. After all, the Americans might think that Prinzel, rather than he, von Igelfeld, represented German philology, and this, frankly, would never do. Quite apart from that, if Prinzel went first, they would never hear the end of it.

'I have no alternative but to go there,' he said to himself. 'And I shall have to make sure that I go before Prinzel. It's simply a matter of duty.'

Von Igelfeld found himself in a difficult position. He could hardly approach any of his American friends and solicit an invitation, particularly after he had so consistently turned them down in the past. And yet the chance that an invitation would arrive of its own accord was extremely slender.

Over coffee at the Institute the next day, he directed a casual question at Professor Dr Detlev Amadeus Unterholzer.

'Tell me, Herr Unterholzer,' he said. 'If you were to want to go to America to give a lecture, how would you . . . well, how would you get yourself invited, so to speak?' Quickly adding: 'Not that I would ever be in such a position myself, but you yourself could be, could you not?'

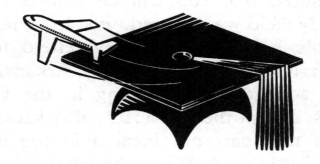

Unterholzer had an immediate answer.

'I should contact the *Deutscher Akademischer Austauschdienst*,' he said. 'I should tell them who I was and I should ask them to arrange a lecture somewhere in America. That is what they are paid to do.'

'I see,' said von Igelfeld. 'That would no doubt save embarrassment.'

'Of course,' said Unterholzer. 'They are experts in finding places for German academics to go and lecture to other people, whether or not they want to hear them. They are very persuasive people. That is how I went to Buenos Aires and gave my lecture there. It really works.'

And indeed it did. The local director of the *Deutscher Akademischer Austauschdienst* was delighted to hear from von Igelfeld the following day and assured him that a scholar of his eminence would be snapped up should he deign to leave Germany. It was only a question of finding the right institution and making the detailed arrangements.

'Rest assured that you will be invited within days,' von Igelfeld was assured. 'Just leave it all in our capable hands.' Thus von Igelfeld found himself arriving in Fayetteville, Arkansas, a charming college town nestling in the Ozark Mountains, seat of the University of Arkansas, or at least of that part not located in the minor campus at Little Rock. When the whole idea was conceived, he had not envisaged going to Arkansas. He had imagined that his destination might be California, or New York, perhaps, but one American state was very much the same as another – at least in von Igelfeld's view, and it really made no difference. The important thing was that he was going to America, and a good two weeks ahead of Prinzel.

Von Igelfeld's host greeted him warmly. They

had insisted that he stay with them, rather than in a hotel, and so von Igelfeld found himself installed in the sleeping porch of a traditional Ozark farmhouse on the edge of the town, the home of Professor R. B. Leflar. After he had unpacked, he and von Igelfeld sat down on the swingseat on the front verandah and discussed his programme. There would be visits to the surrounding area the next day, promised Professor Leflar, and the day after that a set-piece lecture had been planned before an open audience.

That night, after dinner, von Igelfeld retired to his bed and looked out through the gauze-covered porch windows. The house was surrounded by mixed forest, oak trees and sycamores, and their shapes, dark silhouettes, swayed in the breeze. And there, he thought, there's the moon, rising slowly over the trees like a giant lantern. What were they planning for him tomorrow? Would they show him their libraries? Were there manuscripts? What about Leflar's maternal grandfather, the adventurer, Charles Finger? He had been in South America and may have come across some Portuguese manuscripts of note, which could well be in the attic above his very head. Arkansas, it seemed, was rich in possibilities for the philo-logist.

The next morning he ate a hearty breakfast with Professor and Mrs Leflar before they set off.

'We're heading north,' said his host. 'We'll show you a typical hog operation.'

'Most intriguing,' said von Igelfeld. 'I am always interested in . . .' He paused. What was he interested in? Philology? Portuguese verbs? 'I am always interested in everything.'

They drove out of town, following a road that wound up into the hills. It was a gentle landscape – limestone hills which had been softened by the action of the rain; meandering valleys dotted with farmhouses under shady oak trees. Von Igelfeld had not thought of America as being at all like this; there were no dry plains, no glittering Dallas in the distance, no leafy suburbia with neat white houses. This could have been Bavaria, or even Austria.

Suddenly Leflar turned off the road and followed a dusty track leading towards a large, unpainted barn.

'Here we are,' he said. 'They're expecting us.'

The farmer came out and shook von Igelfeld's hand. Von Igelfeld sniffed the air; it was distinctly malodorous.

'This way,' said the farmer. 'The hogs are in here.'

The farmer opened a door in the side of the barn and ushered von Igelfeld inside. For the next half hour, they wandered between rows of large sties, each surmounted by a large sun lamp and each filled with a squealing mass of pigs. The farmer demonstrated the automatic feeding system and showed von Igelfeld the blood-sampling equipment.

'We're mighty careful about viruses here,' he said. 'You'd know all about that.'

Von Igelfeld looked at the farmer. Did pigs get colds, he wondered?

'You have to be careful about viruses,' he agreed. 'I myself always use vitamin C during the winter . . .'

He did not finish. 'You're right,' said the farmer. 'Each pig gets sixty IU vitamin C every morning with its food. And then we give them a shot of B group when they're seven weeks old. Some people are trying a short course of potassium a week before market. What do you think?'

Von Igelfeld shook his head. 'You have to be careful,' he said. 'I would never use potassium myself.'

The farmer listened intently. 'You hear that, Professor Leflar? No potassium. I'm inclined to agree with our visitor. You tell those folks down in Little Rock, no potassium – the Germans recommend against it.'

Leflar nodded. 'Could be,' he said.

An hour later they set off again. After a brief lunch, they made their way to a chicken farm, where von Igelfeld was shown the latest methods of production by a farmer who spoke in such a way that he could understand not one word. Then there was a call at some sort of animal laboratory, which interested von Igelfeld very little. Then home to dinner.

That night, in the silence of his sleeping porch,

von Igelfeld reflected on his day. It had been interesting, in its way, but he wondered why they had chosen to show him all those farms and animals. Animals were all very well; indeed he had once written a small paper on the nature of collective nouns used for groups of animals, but that was about as far as his interest went. Still, this was America, and he assumed that this was what they laid on for all their visitors.

The lecture was to be at six thirty, following a short reception. When von Igelfeld arrived with Leflar the audience was largely assembled, milling about the ante-room of the lecture theatre. Glasses of wine had been provided, and plates of snacks were being circulated by waitresses dressed in black and white.

Everybody seemed keen to talk to von Igelfeld.

'We've all heard about your work,' said one man in a light-weight blue suit. 'In fact, I've got an off-print here which I thought you might care to sign.'

'I'd be happy to do so,' said von Igelfeld. And what about *Portuguese Irregular Verbs*? he reflected. Were there copies even here in Fayetteville, amongst these charming hills?

The man in the blue suit produced a pamphlet from his pocket.

'I was sent this by a colleague in Germany,' he said. 'He thought that I might find it useful. And I sure did.'

Von Igelfeld took the pamphlet. The cover was

unfamiliar; all his off-prints from the *Zeitschrift* were bound in a plain white cover. This one was blue.

He adjusted his reading glasses and looked at the title page.

Further Studies of Canine Pulmonary Efficiency, he read. And then: *by Professor Martin Igelfold, University of Münster.*

Von Igelfeld stared at the page for a moment, his heart a cold stone within him. It was immediately clear to him what had happened. They thought that he was Professor Igelfold, Dean of Veterinary Medicine at Münster. Von Igelfeld knew of Igelfold's existence, as he had seen the remarkably similar name in the newspaper during an anthrax scare. But he had never dreamed that there would be confusion on such a heroic scale! Those foolish, bumbling people at the *Deutscher Akademischer Austauschdienst* had mixed them up and sent him off to lecture on veterinary medicine in Arkansas! It was a situation of such terrible embarrassment that for a moment he hardly dared contemplate it. And the lecture was about to begin, before all these people – these expectant scientists, veterinarians and dog breeders – and he had proposed to talk about modal verbs in the writings of Fernando Pessoa.

Almost without thinking, he signed the pamphlet and returned it to the other man.

'We're so honoured to have you here in Fayetteville,' said the man. 'We understand that you are the world authority on the sausage dog. We are looking forward to what you have to say to us tonight. Sausage dogs are quite popular here. German settlers brought them with them in the late eighteen nineties and have bred them ever since.'

Von Igelfeld stared at him in horror. Sausage dogs! He was expected to talk about sausage dogs, a subject on which he knew absolutely nothing. It was a nightmare; like one of those dreams where you imagine that you are about to take the lead part in a Greek play or where you are sitting down to write an examination in advanced calculus. But he was awake, and it was really happening.

Leflar was at his side now.

'Almost time,' he said. 'Should I ask people to move into the hall?'

'Not yet,' said von Igelfeld, looking about him desperately. 'I have so many colleagues yet to meet.'

He detached himself from Leflar and made his way over to a knot of people standing near the door. This proved to be a group of veterinary surgeons who welcomed him to their circle and refilled his glass from a bottle of wine which one of them was holding.

It was in this group that one of the guests drew him aside and engaged him in distinctly unsettling conversation.

'I was sorry to read about your death,' said the guest.

Von Igelfeld looked at him in astonishment.

'My death?'

'Yes,' said the guest. 'There was a small item in the *International Veterinary Review* this week reporting the very recent death of Professor Igelfold. There was a glowing obituary.'

Von Igelfeld stared glassily at the man before him, who was surveying him over his drink.

'I did not read it,' he said weakly.

'Not surprising,' said the man. 'One rarely has the pleasure of reading one's own obituary.'

Von Igelfeld laughed, mopping his brow with his handkerchief.

'Very amusing,' he said. 'And you are so right!'

'So this *is* a posthumous lecture,' said the man.

'Well,' said von Igelfeld. 'It would appear to be something of that sort.'

The man looked pensive. 'I must say that you don't look at all like your photograph. They published one with the obituary, you know.'

Von Igelfeld gripped at the stem of his glass. 'The camera is often deceptive, I find.'

'You were a smaller man in the photograph,' went on the other. 'Not nearly so tall.'

'I see,' said von Igelfeld icily. 'A smaller photograph, perhaps? Anyway, do you not know that in Germany we sometimes publish obituaries *before* a person's demise. It happens quite often. This is because we Germans are so efficient. An early obituary means that there is never a backlog. That, I suspect, is the explanation.'

11

There was a silence. Then von Igelfeld spoke again.

'You must excuse me,' he said. 'I am feeling rather tired.'

'Quite understandable,' muttered the man. 'In the circumstances.'

But von Igelfeld did not hear him. He had moved away and was looking about him. The simplest solution was to escape, to vanish entirely. If he managed to get out of the hall he could summon a taxi, go back to the Leflar house, creep in through the back and reclaim his belongings. Then he could make his way to the airport and await the first flight out of town, wherever it happened to be going.

The front door was impossible. Everybody would see him leaving and somebody was bound to come after him to enquire where he was going. But there was another door at the side of the room, a door out of which it looked much easier to sneak. He moved over towards it, smiling at people as he walked past, nodding his head in acknowledgement of their greetings. Then, having reached the door, he discreetly turned the handle and pushed against it.

'Oh, there you are,' said Leflar. 'Is everything all right?'

'I am very well,' said von Igelfeld. 'I was just trying . . .' His voice faded away.

Leflar glanced anxiously at his watch . . .

'We don't have much time,' he said. 'The hall

has to be used for another purpose in twenty-five minutes.'

'Please don't hurry,' said von Igelfeld. 'The real point of these meetings is that there should be personal contact and I am making sure that this happens by talking to all these excellent people.'

A few minutes later, von Igelfeld looked out over the faces of his audience. They had enjoyed the reception, and the supply of wine had been liberal. He, too, had taken several glasses and had recovered after the shock of discovering that he was dead. Now it now seemed to him that to talk for – what time remained? – ten minutes at the most about sausage dogs would not be an impossible task. And by now he had remembered that Zimmermann himself had been in such a situation some years before, when he had been mistaken for another Zimmermann and had been obliged to deliver a lecture on developments in exhaust systems, a subject of which he was completely ignorant. And yet had he not done so, and with distinction? With such distinction, indeed, that the resulting paper had been published in the *Karlsruher Forum fur Moderne Auspuffkonstruktion?* If Zimmermann could do it, then surely he could do so too.

'The sausage dog,' he began, 'is a remarkable dog. It differs from other dogs in respect of its shape, which is similar to that of a sausage. It belongs to that genus of dogs marked out by their proximity to the ground. In most cases this is because of the shortness of the legs. If a dog has short legs, we have found that the body is almost invariably close to the ground. Yet this does not prevent the sausage dog from making its way about its business with considerable despatch.'

He glanced at his watch. One minute had passed, leaving nine minutes to go. There would be one minute, or perhaps two, for thanks at the end, which meant that he now had to speak for no more than seven minutes. But what more was there to say about sausage dogs? Were they good hunting dogs? He believed they were. Perhaps he could say something about the role of the sausage

dog in the rural economy, how they had their place and how unwise it was to introduce new, untested breeds.

This went down well with the audience, and there were murmurs of agreement from corners of the room. Emboldened, von Igelfeld moved on to the topic of whether there should be restrictions on the free movement of sausage dogs. Should sausage dog breeders not be allowed to export animals with as few restrictions as possible? Again the audience agreed with von Igelfeld when he said that this was a good idea.

There were several other points before it was time to stop. After thanking Leflar and the University of Arkansas, von Igelfeld sat down, to thunderous applause.

Leflar leant over to von Igelfeld as the sound of clapping filled the room.

'Well done,' he said. 'That went down very well. Guest speakers are sometimes far too technical for an open lecture like this. You hit just the right note.'

Von Igelfeld nodded gravely.

'I hope I lived up to expectations,' he said modestly.

'Oh you did,' said Leflar. 'It was a resounding success. Even if you were somewhat brief.'

From his seat on the aeroplane, von Igelfeld looked down at the Ozarks as they became smaller and smaller beneath him. It was a good place, America, and Arkansas was a good state. He had been invited to return, but how could he, particularly when the news of Professor Igelfold's death became widespread? Besides, he reflected, he had nothing further to say about sausage dogs; indeed he had already said more than enough.

A LEG TO STAND ON

Arkanas had been a welcome diversion for von Igelfeld. He had felt quite exhausted before embarking on the trip but had returned entirely refreshed, ready to face the pressing burdens of daily life at the Institute for Romance Philology in Regensburg.

The reason for von Igelfeld's fatigue before his departure was the effort that he had been obliged to expend – at very short notice – on the writing of a radio talk on Portuguese orthography. He had taken great care with this talk, and the programme had eventually been broadcast by German State Radio at five o'clock on a particularly wet Thursday evening.

Von Igelfeld had been pleased with his talk, which he felt had achieved the requisite delicate balance between the rival theories on the issue. Some weeks later he had telephoned the producer to establish whether there had been any reaction to what he had said.

The producer had sounded evasive.

'It's rather difficult to gauge reaction,' he had said. 'That's a tricky slot on Thursday evening. Many people are still on their way home from work.'

'I know that,' snapped von Igelfeld. 'But there are still plenty of people at home. They could have listened.'

'Well . . .' said the producer. 'It's a difficult time. And the audience research reports . . .'

'Is that some sort of survey?' interrupted von Igelfeld. 'Does it show how many people listened?'

'Well,' said the producer, hesitantly. 'I'm afraid it was not all that encouraging. In fact, we had a negative result. Apparently nobody tuned in at all. Nobody heard you.'

There was a silence at the other end of the line.

'Nobody?'

'Of course, these things are often unreliable.'

'I should think they are,' said von Igelfeld. 'I, for one, listened. And then there's my colleague, Professor Dr Unterholzer. He listened, I can assure you.'

'There you are,' said the producer. 'That's something.'

In fact, unbeknown to von Igelfeld, Unterholzer had not listened. He had fully intended to do so, having been reminded by von Igelfeld on four separate occasions of the time of the broadcast, but had become so absorbed in a musical concert that he had forgotten to switch stations. So, as far as anybody knew, von Igelfeld was the only person in Germany to hear his own talk.

But the radio broadcast seemed distant now, and other challenges were on the horizon. There was the Berlin meeting on Celtic philology – always a major date in von Igelfeld's calendar – and there was a lecture to prepare for Salzburg. And then there was, of course, the work which had to be done on *The Portuguese Pluperfect*, the book on which von Igelfeld had been working for the last few years and which, in the opinion of all those who had glimpsed the manuscript, was sure to become a worthy successor to *Portuguese Irregular Verbs* itself.

When the letter arrived from Professor R. B. Leflar, von Igelfeld opened it almost absent-mindedly. He was aware of the fact that it bore an American stamp; American stamps, he had observed, always showed people *doing* things, whereas German stamps were designed not to excite people too much and were somehow more appropriate. He was reflecting on this when he noticed the fateful post-mark: *Fayetteville, Arkansas*. Had he seen that, he would have known at once the authorship of the letter.

'*Dear Professor von Igelfeld,*' the letter began. '*I would never have imagined, when we said farewell to one another in Arkansas barely nine months ago, that I should be seeing you so soon. But I now find myself having to come to Germany and I should therefore*

18

like to take you up on your kind invitation to visit Regensburg . . .'

Von Igelfeld smiled as he read the letter. He had enjoyed Professor Leflar's company and the thought of showing him around Regensburg was an attractive one. He would take him down to the river and, if the weather was fine, perhaps they could . . . He stopped. The awful thought had occurred that as far as Leflar was concerned, von Igelfeld was still a professor of veterinary medicine and the world's leading authority on the sausage dog. He had not disabused him of this misconception, although he should perhaps have done this right at the outset. But once he had allowed matters to persist and had delivered the lecture on sausage dogs, then it had been too late. Now it was impossible to confess that he had enjoyed the hospitality of his hosts in Fayetteville under entirely false pretences.

That would not have been too troubling had it not been for the fact of Leflar's impending arrival. It would be impossible to maintain the pretence of being a professor of veterinary medicine right here in Regensburg, where everybody knew that he was a Romance philologist. But did he have any alternative? It would be simply too embarrassing to tell the truth now, to confess to an utter ignorance of sausage dogs; he would simply have to brazen it out and pretend for the two days of Leflar's visit that he was, indeed, what he so patently was not. It was not an appealing prospect.

'I shall not be coming into the Institute next week,' he said to Unterholzer. 'I shall be . . .'

Unterholzer looked at him expectantly.

'In Berlin?' he asked, a note of jealousy creeping into his voice. 'Has somebody asked you to go to Berlin?'

Von Igelfeld shook his head. It was typical of Unterholzer to be immoderately inquisitive. How von Igelfeld spent his time had nothing to do with him and there was no call for him to reveal such vulgar curiosity.

Unterholzer persisted. 'Munich?' he pressed. 'Wiesbaden?'

Von Igelfeld felt the irritation well up within him. 'I shall be right here in Regensburg,' he snapped. 'I shall just not be coming into the Institute. That is all.'

Unterholzer was silent. He knew that von Igelfeld was concealing something, but short of following him about, which he clearly could not do, there was little chance of his discovering what it was. For von Igelfeld's part, he realised that silence might have been more advisable: if he had simply said nothing, then Unterholzer may never even have noticed his absence. As it was, he would have to make sure that their paths did not cross during Leflar's visit. Unterholzer was noted for his insecurity. He would surely interpret the presence of a mysterious stranger in von Igelfeld's company as some sort of threat to himself and could be counted on to try to find out his identity.

The essential difficulty was that life was unfair, and Unterholzer was one of those who was destined to play second fiddle, or worse. He had the worst office in the Institute; his book was all but ignored by everybody in the field; and he rarely received invitations to lecture anywhere of the remotest interest. His Buenos Aires invitation had come merely because they could get nobody else to attend the conference, although von Igelfeld had generously refrained from telling him that. He had hinted it, though, but Unterholzer, with typical lack of insight, had failed to read his meaning. Poor Unterholzer! reflected von Igelfeld. What it must be to be such a failure and to have so little . . .

Von Igelfeld's reveries came to an abrupt end. To have so little in this life and yet to have received – oh, the sheer injustice of it – a medal from the Portuguese Government! A medal which must have been intended for himself, von Igelfeld, not for the hopelessly obscure Unterholzer. All he had ever done for the Lusophile world had been to pen a badly received volume on the Portuguese imperfect subjunctive. This was a book which was barely fit to rest on the same shelf as *Portuguese Irregular Verbs*, and yet some misguided official in Lisbon has recommended the award of a medal! It was quite clear to von Igelfeld that the medals of this world were pinned on quite the wrong chests, just as were the metaphorical barriers inevitably placed in quite the wrong place.

Leflar arrived on a Tuesday. It was a wonderful spring day and the air was sharp and invigorating.

'A peach of a day!' the American visitor remarked as von Igelfeld met him at the railway station. 'The sort of day that in Arkansas makes us go hippety-hop!'

'Hippety-hop?' said von Igelfeld, slightly taken aback. 'Oh yes. We Germans like to go hippety-hop too on days like this.'

They travelled by taxi to the Hotel Angst, where von Igelfeld had booked Leflar in for the two nights of his stay.

'I am sure that you'll be very comfortable here,' he explained. 'The Institute always uses this hotel for its visitors. We put Professor Hutmann here last time. He is an old friend of mine from student days in Heidelberg.'

Leflar looked surprised. 'Heidelberg? I didn't realise they taught veterinary medicine at Heidelberg.'

Von Igelfeld froze. Leflar had scarcely arrived and he had already made a bad mistake.

'Heidelberg?' he said quickly. 'Who said anything about Heidelberg?'

'You did,' said Leflar. 'You referred to being a student at Heidelberg. You said you studied at Heidelberg.'

'I did not,' said von Igelfeld. 'You must have

misheard me. I said that Professor Hutmann was an old friend, in Heidelberg, from student days. That is, we were friends, in student days, but now he is in Heidelberg.'

'So,' he went on quickly. 'I shall leave you here for a while, but I shall be back soon to take you out to lunch. In the afternoon, I can show you round the town.'

They bade farewell and von Igelfeld made his way home, deep in thought. If matters were difficult at this stage, then how much more complicated they would become when it came to taking Leflar to the Veterinary Institute tomorrow, as he had requested.

Tuesday afternoon was a considerable success. Leflar enjoyed a walk in the hills above the town and they both ate a hearty meal in a small inn on the river. But von Igelfeld's pleasure at his friend's delight in the beauty of Regensburg was tinged with apprehension. The moment was fast approaching when he would have to present himself at the Veterinary Institute and join Leflar in the tour which had been arranged for him. That, at least, had been easy. He had simply informed the Director of the Institute that a personal friend, a prominent American expert in animal health, was visiting and that he would like to show him the Institute. The Director had promised to conduct the tour himself and had invited von Igelfeld to join them. What would happen if the Director made some remark which indicated that von Igelfeld was an outsider from a totally different part of the university? And would Leflar expect von Igelfeld to join in any debate engaged in by himself and the Director? If that happened, there would be no alternative but to claim an urgent appointment elsewhere.

By the time they arrived at the Institute, von Igelfeld was already beginning to feel a cold chill of dread. But when the Director, a charming man wearing a neat bow-tie, welcomed them both, his fear dissipated somewhat. The Director addressed all his technical remarks to Leflar and all that von Igelfeld had to do was to nod in agreement.

'We're engaged in a major programme of research on the genetics of degenerative disease in turkeys,' said the Director, and von Igelfeld nodded, as if to convey that he, too, was heavily involved.

'It's an important topic,' said Leflar.

'Yes,' agreed von Igelfeld. 'Very important. From the . . . from the . . . turkey point of view.'

The Director threw him a glance. Now they moved on to the laboratories, where humming centrifuges and bubbling flasks attested to a high level of research activity.

'Mg_2 H_2O + $HgSO_4$,' explained the Director, pointing to a vat of curiously coloured powder.

'H_2?' asked Leflar.

'$MgCO_2$,' responded the Director.

'O,' said von Igelfeld. 'H.'

'O?' asked Leflar.

Von Igelfeld stroked his chin. 'Perhaps.'

'Definitely,' interjected the Director. 'H_2O + $NaCl_3$.'

They moved on to the physiology laboratory, where Leflar found a great deal to interest him. Von Igelfeld felt relaxed now; there seemed to be no reason why Leflar should suspect anything and all that remained was to join the Director for a social cup of coffee in his office. That, it transpired, was even easier, as the conversation was restricted to small talk and a discussion of the relative merits of Fayetteville and Regensburg. Then the Director took his leave, as he had a meeting to attend, leaving von Igelfeld to escort Leflar towards the front door. And it was at this point that the movement of the planets brought about what, for von Igelfeld, was a thoroughly disagreeable concatenation of events.

Nemesis took the form of a young man, evidently a student, who suddenly dashed out of a door and seized von Igelfeld's arm.

'Herr Professor,' he said. 'You must come in immediately. We've had a casualty brought in to the clinic. I can't find Dr Steenbock and the staff in the lab said that I should ask you.'

Von Igelfeld found himself being ushered into a small room, the stark white walls of which were lit by a large overhead light. There was a high table with a stainless steel top and stretched out on that, connected by a tube to a cylinder of gas, was the anaesthetised form of a sausage dog.

'He was brought in a few minutes ago,' said the young man. 'One of his legs has been crushed by a car. I've just developed the X-rays.'

He flicked the switch of a light box, illuminating a ghostly picture of bones and tissue.

'The trouble is,' went on the young man. 'I'm only a third year student. Dr Steenbock would normally supervise me. I'm not allowed to do unsupervised surgery yet.'

Von Igelfeld looked about him wildly. This was worse – far worse – than his ordeal in Arkansas. He was utterly cornered. But he would cope with the situation, just as he had coped with everything that had gone before. This was no time for defeat.

'Well, I'll just stand back and let you get on with it,' said Leflar helpfully. 'I do very little small animal surgery. I'll just watch.'

26

'You do it,' von Igelfeld to the student. 'I'm sure that you'll be fine.'

'But what shall I do?' asked the student.

Von Igelfeld craned his neck to examine the X-ray.

'The leg is broken,' he said. 'Look at this.'

'Yes,' said the student. 'It's a badly impacted fracture.'

'Then we shall have to amputate it,' said von Igelfeld. 'Cut it off.'

The student nodded. Then, opening a drawer below the table he extracted a scalpel and a large, terrifying instrument that looked to all intents and purposes like a pair of garden secateurs.

'Go ahead,' said von Igelfeld.

The student took the rear leg of the dog in his hand and made an incision. Bright canine blood appeared like a line of tiny flowers, but that was only the beginning. Soon the deeper structures were exposed and then, with a firm snip, the bone was cut neatly by the secateurs. It did not take long for the wound to be sewn up and there, in a metal dish, lay a small, detached leg.

'Good,' said von Igelfeld. 'Well done.'

The student leaned forward to peer at the X-ray. Suddenly he groaned.

'Oh no, Herr Professor! That was the wrong leg!'

Von Igelfeld looked at the plate. The broken leg was on the right, as was the leg which had been removed, but now, looking more closely, it was clearly in the front.

'Take the right one off,' he said sharply. 'You have been very careless.'

The student reached again for his instruments and began the process of cutting into the injured leg. Again there was a bloodflow, quickly stemmed with a smouldering cauteriser, and soon another leg joined the one already in the dish.

'Good,' said von Igelfeld, emboldened. 'I shall now assist you, in order to give you more confidence.'

He reached forward and took the scalpel from the student's shaking hand. But as he did so, he slipped, and the sharp blade plunged deep into the remaining back leg. There was a fountain of blood and the student gave a shout.

'You've severed an artery, Herr Professor!'

'Take the leg off then,' said von Igelfeld. 'Hurry.'

Again the amputation procedure went ahead, leaving the poor sausage dog with a sole leg, in the front. Leflar, who had been watching intently, had been silent, save for a sharp intake of breath at the more dramatic events.

'Poor dog,' he said at last. 'He's not going to be able to get around very well with only one leg.'

Von Igelfeld looked at the sadly diminished sausage dog.

'He can roll,' he pronounced. 'He will be able to get around by rolling.'

In the meantime, the student who had gone outside to sterilise the instruments had returned.

'The owner is waiting outside, Herr Professor,'

he said. 'Could you explain to him what has happened?'

Von Igelfeld nodded. 'I shall tell him that it has been necessary to perform extensive surgery,' he said. 'Bring him in and I shall tell him what we have done.'

The student retreated and returned a few moments later with the anxious owner.

It was Unterholzer.

ON THE COUCH

Relations between Professor Dr Moritz-Maria von Igelfeld, author of *Portuguese Irregular Verbs*, and Professor Dr Detlev Amadeus Unterholzer, author of a considerably less well-regarded work on the Portuguese imperfect subjunctive, were somewhat strained. Nothing was said, of course, but it was clear to von Igelfeld that Unterholzer continued to harbour a grudge against him over the unfortunate incident involving his dog. It was von Igelfeld's view that he was entirely blameless in this affair, and that if anyone bore any responsibility for it, then Unterholzer himself might be the most appropriate candidate. After all, it was his own failure to supervise the dog adequately that had left it free to run out into the road and collide with a passing motorist. Unterholzer should feel ashamed of this; if people failed to take adequate care of their sausage dogs, then accidents were only to be expected. And anyway, von Igelfeld reflected, the outcome could have been infinitely worse. It was true that the dog had lost three legs in the incident, but the Veterinary Institute had gone out of its way to fit it with a prosthetic appliance that appeared to be working very well. An elaborate harness was secured round the dog's body and attached to this were three small wheels. By using its remaining leg as a paddle, the dog could propel itself on its wheels and get anywhere it wished to get. Only very occasionally did the system not work, as had happened once or twice on a hill, when the dog had got out of control and careered down the pavement on its tiny wheels, unable to stop itself, and had ended up on a lawn or in a bush. But these were minor inconveniences, and it was quite wrong for Unterholzer to maintain a coldness in his dealings with his senior colleague; Romance philology was too small a field to allow for animosity, at least with regard to personal disputes. Academic questions were another matter, of course; the issues there were real and it was sometimes inevitable that one had to be direct in one's criticisms of a colleague's misconceptions.

'I trust that all is going well, Herr Unterholzer,' remarked von Igelfeld one morning, in an attempt to break the ice.

'In part,' replied Unterholzer. 'Some matters are progressing well, but there are others which are not so satisfactory.'

There was silence for a few moments, as Unterholzer awaited von Igelfeld's response to the challenge. But none came.

'What I mean,' went on Unterholzer, 'is that it takes a toll to be looking after a handicapped dog. There are so many things to worry about. Such a dog might become stuck in the mud, for example, if one's dog happens to have wheels, that is. Only yesterday I had to oil him. One does not usually have to oil a dog, I think.'

Von Igelfeld bit his lip. It really was too much, this stream of unspoken accusations.

'Indeed,' he said, in a steely tone. 'Supervising a dog is very demanding. One would not want one's dog, while unsupervised, or negligently supervised perhaps, to run out into the traffic, would one, Herr Unterholzer?'

Unterholzer said nothing, but turned away and busied himself with some task. Von Igelfeld, for his part, was pleased with the way he had managed to turn the encounter to his advantage. Unterholzer would think twice now before he raised the question of the sausage dog again.

There was no further word from Unterholzer for two weeks. They passed one another in the corridor, and uttered courteous greetings, but no pleasantries were exchanged. Von Igelfeld was content to leave matters as they stood: if Unterholzer wished to smoulder, let him do so. He would only make himself look ridiculous in the eyes of a world which, if it were ever to discover the true background to the affair, would certainly side with von Igelfeld.

When Unterholzer eventually struck, it was with a suddenness that took von Igelfeld entirely by surprise. The *Zeitschrift*, which had previously been edited by von Igelfeld, but which was now edited from Frankfurt, arrived on the first day of every third month. Von Igelfeld had a personal subscription and enjoyed nothing more than taking his copy home on the day of its arrival and settling down to read it in his study over a glass of Madeira wine. It was, in many respects, the highlight of his existence: to savour the unadulterated pleasure of at least four articles on Romance philology, together with at least ten pages of book reviews, and several pages of *Notes and Queries*. Usually he finished his first reading of the journal that evening, and would return to it over the following days, after he had mulled over the contents.

On this occasion, he sat down with the Madeira and the review, and fixed his eye upon the Contents page. There was an article by Professor Dr Dr Mannhein on particles. (*A treat!* thought von Igelfeld.) There was a review essay on an important new etymological dictionary of Spanish, and . . . He faltered, the glass of Madeira toppling dangerously to one side.

It was there in black and white, the letters imprinted on the page with all the awful finality of names inscribed in some awful monument to an atrocity: *Irregular Verbs: Flaws in the von Igelfeld Hypothesis.* Von Igelfeld gasped, and gasped again when he saw what followed: by Professor Dr Dr Detlev Amadeus Unterholzer (Regensburg).

With fumbling hands he turned to the first page of the article and began to read.

'*Since the publication of the controversial* Portuguese Irregular Verbs *by Professor Dr Moritz-Maria von Igelfeld, scholars of Romance philology have been questioning some of the basic assumptions as to the behaviour of the indicative in its irregular manifestations. The growing band of those who are unconvinced by the tentative hypothesis advanced by von Igelfeld have begun to suggest that third person mutations happened later than von Igelfeld naïvely assumes . . .*'

It was almost too much for von Igelfeld to bear. With his heart hammering within him, he struggled to the end of the article, reeling at the subtle digs which virtually every sentence seemed to contain. Not only was he, according to Unterholzer, 'naïve' (page 34), but he was also 'misguided' (page 36), 'misinformed' (page 37) and 'potentially meretricious' (page 39).

He finished the article and laid the *Zeitschrift* down on the table beside his chair, next to the untouched glass of Madeira. He had never before – not once – been attacked in print. The reviews of *Portuguese Irregular Verbs* had been unanimously favourable; at conferences, colleagues had tripped over one another in the race to compliment him on his papers; and Zimmermann himself had never – not on one single occasion – uttered anything but praise of his work. And now here was Unterholzer – Unterholzer! – daring to question his theories, clothing himself, it would seem, in the support of a so-called 'growing band' of those unconvinced of his hypothesis. Who was in this 'growing band' on whose behalf Unterholzer purported to speak? Was Prinzel involved? Von Igelfeld had spoken to him only three weeks ago and there had been no indication of doubts as to the hypothesis. No, it was more likely that Unterholzer spoke for nobody but himself and had merely invented the support of others, in the same way as those who are unsure of themselves may use the first person plural when they express a view.

For the rest of the evening, von Igelfeld considered his response. One possibility was to confront Unterholzer and to ask him to explain himself. Another was to appear so wounded by the remarks that he would induce in Unterholzer a feeling of guilt for his appalling betrayal. And finally, he could just ignore the article altogether and pretend that he had not noticed the attack. The first and the second options were fraught with risks. He was unwilling to engage with Unterholzer in a point for point refutation of the criticisms he had made – to do that would be to lend to them a gravity that they patently did not deserve. And if he appeared wounded, then Unterholzer would have the satisfaction of knowing that the ridiculous barbs had struck home, which was presumably what he wanted. This left him the option of dignified silence, which he knew he was capable of managing. He had often shown a dignified silence in the past when faced with Unterholzer and his doings, and so all that he would have do would be rather more dignified and silent than usual.

Over the next few days, whenever von Igelfeld saw Unterholzer in the Institute, he merely nodded gravely in his direction and passed on. Unterholzer tried to speak to him on one occasion, but von Igelfeld pretended to be deep in thought and not to notice him. He thought, but could not be certain, that Unterholzer looked worried, and this gave him considerable pleasure. He could continue to keep his distance – for years if necessary – until Unterholzer knocked on his door with an unconditional apology. And even then, it might take some time before an apology could be accepted, so grave was the offence which Unterholzer had committed.

Yet as the days passed, von Igelfeld found himself increasingly puzzled by Unterholzer's apparent ability to endure the Coventry to which he had been consigned. Unterholzer was seen laughing and joking with some of the junior assistants and was, in von Igelfeld's hearing, described by the Librarian as being 'in remarkably good spirits'. It seemed to von Igelfeld that his colleague had acquired an extraordinary new confidence. Not only had he shown the temerity to criticise *Portuguese Irregular Verbs* in the columns of the *Zeitschrift*, but he seemed to have overcome his previous hesitance and inadequacy in his everyday dealings with his colleagues. This was disturbing; if Unterholzer were to start throwing his weight around, then the Institute would become a distinctly less attractive place. Nobody wanted Unterholzer's opinions on anything, and it was highly undesirable that he should see fit to give them.

Von Igelfeld decided to take the matter up with the Librarian, who had always enjoyed a close relationship with Unterholzer.

'Professor Unterholzer seems in very good form these days,' he remarked. 'He's rather more confident than before, would you not say?'

'Dear Professor Unterholzer!' said the Librarian. 'He's certainly more forthcoming than he used to be. But then that's psychoanalysis for you!'

Von Igelfeld narrowed his eyes. 'Psychoanalysis?' he said. 'Do you mean that Professor Unterholzer is undergoing analysis?'

'Yes,' said the Librarian. 'In fact, I can take some of the credit for it. I recommended it to him and arranged for him to meet Dr Hubertoffel. He's a very good analyst – one of the best, I believe.'

Von Igelfeld made a noncommittal sound and brought the discussion to an end. Stalking off to his office, he began to ponder the implications of

37

what he had been told. *Confidence! Psychoanalysis! Dr Hubertoffel!* It was all profoundly unsettling. He was used to the order of things as they were, and the thought of a liberated Unterholzer, free of the manifold inadequacies which up to now had made his company just bearable, was extremely disturbing. He would have to find out more about this Dr Hubertoffel and see whether there was any way of restraining the baneful influence which he seemed to be having on Unterholzer's life. If this involved a visit to Dr Hubertoffel himself, then von Igelfeld was prepared to do even that. He had always harboured the gravest mistrust of both Freudians and Freemasons, whom he regarded as being inextricably linked, but the task ahead of him had now acquired an urgency which could not be ignored: the reputation of the Institute, and that of *Portuguese Irregular Verbs* itself, could depend on bringing Unterholzer to heel before even more damaging attacks could be made. To this end, he was even prepared to wander into the Freudian cage itself and deal with whatever lion figures may be found within. Dr Max Augustus Hubertoffel of the *Hubertoffel Klinik für Neurosen und Psychopathologie* looked every inch a man who was suited to his calling. He was a slight, dapper man, with slickly parted hair, a Viennese bow-tie, and carefully polished black patent-leather shoes. His consulting rooms, discreetly tucked away in a quiet street in Regensburg's professional quarter, were

reached by a winding stair that culminated in a
dark green door. Onto this door had been screwed
Dr Hubertoffel's brass plate into which von
Igelfeld, recovering his breath from the stairs, now
peered and saw his own face staring back.

Once admitted to the analyst's sanctum, von
Igelfeld found the doctor looking at him politely
over his desk. Von Igelfeld was asked a few questions and his answers were noted down by Dr
Hubertoffel in a large black notebook. Then the
latter gestured to a green baize-covered couch and
invited von Igelfeld to lie down.

The author of *Portuguese Irregular Verbs* settled
himself on the couch. It was comfortable, but not
so comfortable as to be soporific.

'You may close your eyes, if you wish,' said Dr
Hubertoffel. 'Some analysands prefer to do that,
although there is always the danger of sleep if you
do.'

Von Igelfeld found himself wondering if Unterholzer closed his eyes during analysis, or whether he gazed up at Dr Hubertoffel's ceiling and plotted. Indeed, it was quite possible that the idea of attacking *Portuguese Irregular Verbs* had been conceived on this very couch – oh hateful, hateful thought!

'You will have heard of free association,' said Dr Hubertoffel. 'I find it a useful tool in the discovery of what is troubling a patient. Then, on the basis of this knowledge, I know what I should look out for during the process of analysis. The mind, you see, is full of dark furniture.'

Von Igelfeld gave a start. Dark furniture? Was his own mind full of such a thing? Perhaps it was unwise to undertake analysis, even for the purpose of equipping himself to deal with Unterholzer. If the furniture of the mind was dark, then perhaps it would be best to leave it where it was – in the shadows.

'So,' said Dr Hubertoffel. '*The sea.*'

'The sea?' asked von Igelfeld.

'Yes. I say *the sea* and you tell me what comes into your mind.'

'The sea,' said von Igelfeld.

'No,' said Dr Hubertoffel, patiently. 'I said *the sea*. You tell me what you envisaged.'

'I thought of the sea,' said von Igelfeld. 'That's why I replied the sea when you said the sea.'

Dr Hubertoffel tapped his pencil on the edge of his notebook. 'You must think of something else,' he said. 'Don't be too literal. I'll try again. *Father.*'

'Whiskers,' said von Igelfeld.

'Good,' said Dr Hubertoffel. 'That's a very good reply. Your father had whiskers, I take it.'

'No,' said von Igelfeld. 'But other boys' fathers had them.'

'*Oedipus*,' went on Dr Hubertoffel.

'Mother. No, uncle.'

The psychoanalyst nodded. 'Excellent. Now: *Scissors*.'

'The Suck-a-Thumb Man,' said von Igelfeld. 'You'll remember him from *The Struwelpeter*. He's the man who came to cut off the thumbs of the children who sucked them. I was very frightened of him.'

'And still are, perhaps?' ventured Dr Hubertoffel. 'The shades of the nursery are apt to linger. But let us move on. *Id*.'

'Darkness. Inner me.'

'Excellent. *Sausage*.'

'Dog.'

'*Dog*?'

'Sausage.'

'*Sausage dog*.'

'When I was a boy,' said von Igelfeld, a little later, 'we used to live in Austria, where my grandfather had an estate near Graz. I lived there from the age of six until I was fifteen. Then I was sent to a military academy in Germany. I was very sad to leave Austria and I remember leaning out of the window to catch a last glimpse of my parents and my Uncle Oedipus as they stood on the platform waving to the train. I saw my father raise his hand and then lower it to place it on my mother's shoulder as if to comfort her.'

'Or possibly to reassert ownership,' interjected Dr Hubertoffel.

'My mother turned away and walked back towards our car and I put my head back in the carriage. I was only fifteen, you see, and I had never been away from home. Now I was on my way to the military academy and had no idea of what to expect. I had read *The Young Torless*, of course, and I feared that this was what I was in for. So I sat in my seat and stared dumbly out of the window.

'When I arrived at the school, I was shown to my place in the dormitory. There were forty other boys, all living in the same long room, all engaged in various initiation rituals, whipping one another with wet towels or exchanging blood-brotherhood vows. Several were cutting into one another's hands with blades, in order to mingle blood.

'I was at a loss. There seemed something strange

about the dormitory. There were forty boys, but only twenty beds. We had to share, you see.

'I turned to the boy with whom I had been detailed to share. He was sitting at the end of the bed, gazing glumly at his boots.

'I asked him if he had a nurse at home, and he said that he had just left her. She was a girl called Hysteria, who came from a Bavarian farm, but who was a very good nurse. They had only one bed in the nursery, and he had shared with her. Now he had to share with me, and he was desolate.'

Dr Hubertoffel was listening avidly. 'This is extremely interesting material,' he said, scribbling furiously. 'I am fascinated by this. It is all very pathological.'

Von Igelfeld closed his eyes. It was easier to make up stories with one's eyes closed, he found.

'I survived that first night, although the sobbing of my bed companion largely prevented me from getting any sleep. Then, the next morning, after we had all been forced to take a cold shower, which we shared, our lessons began. The school was very interested in the Franco-Prussian War and devoted many lessons to it. Apart from that, we were taught very little.'

'And were the masters cruel?' asked Dr Hubertoffel.

'Immensely cruel,' said von Igelfeld. 'They used to take great pleasure in devising fresh tortures for the boys, and some of the boys simply could not stand it. Those were the ones who ran away. Sometimes they were returned, and punished all the more. Sometimes they got away and we never heard of them again. I longed to be one of them. But I did not have the courage to leave and, besides, one of the larger boys had cut the soles off my boots to affix to his. I could not have got very far with boots without soles. But there was another reason, too. I was protecting a boy who was being ruthlessly bullied. I had rescued him from his tormentors, but now he relied on me to look after him. If I deserted him, it would be like throwing him to the wolves.'

'Tell me about this boy,' said Dr Hubertoffel.

'He was called Unterholzer,' said von Igelfeld. 'Detlev Amadeus Unterholzer. At least, I think that was his name.'

Von Igelfeld could see that what he had just said had had a marked effect on Dr Hubertoffel.

'Unterholzer?' asked the doctor. 'You protected this . . . this Unterholzer?'

'Yes,' said von Igelfeld. 'He was a very unhappy boy. He had been sent to the military academy by his parents, who hoped that the discipline of such a place would cure him of his dreadful lies. But it did not work, and he continued to be unable to tell truth from falsehood. The other boys did not like this – we had this strict code of honour, you see – and they responded by bullying him. I was the only one to defend him.'

Dr Hubertoffel stared at von Igelfeld.

'So he lied all the time?' he said, eventually.

'Everything he said was untrue,' said von Igelfeld. 'And I suspect it is just the same today. Such people do not really change, do they?'

Dr Hubertoffel thought for a moment. 'Usually not,' he said, gravely. 'Such behaviour indicates a fundamental personality disorder and there is very little we can do about that. Even psychoanalysis is of little help.'

'That's very sad,' said von Igelfeld. 'It must be a great disappointment to you to have patients of that sort.' Adding hurriedly: 'That is, if you do have any like that.'

He left the consulting room shortly afterwards, feeling immensely pleased with himself. He was sure that he had completely derailed Unterholzer's analysis; Dr Hubertoffel had become virtually silent after he had mentioned Unterholzer. He was probably seething with anger that Unterholzer had misled him during the analysis; to sit there and write down all the lies – just as a judge has to do in court – must be a difficult experience.

He walked out into the street. It was a fine evening and he had decided to walk home. Analysis was extraordinary, he reflected. He had gone in feeling somewhat gloomy and had come out feeling quite optimistic. He looked up at the cloudless evening sky and smiled with satisfaction. Unterholzer's little plans would be spiked now; Dr Hubertoffel may have given him the confidence to launch an attack on *Portuguese Irregular Verbs*, but where would that confidence be once he had lost the support of the psychoanalyst?

He walked past a bookshop window and glanced in. There was a display of new academic titles. *The Economy of the Sudanese Uplands* – extremely dull, he thought. *The Upanishads Reviewed* – more promising. Then: *Truth: a Philosophical Defence.*

He paused. Truth. He was on the side of truth, and always had been: it would need no defending while he was around. And was not the motto of the von Igelfelds *Truth Always*? His gaze shifted from the book to his own reflection in the glass of the window, and at that moment an awful pang of guilt shook him. He was looking at the face of a liar!

Von Igelfeld stood stock still. He had done a terrible, dreadful thing. He had walked into the consulting rooms of that poor Freudian and had told him a whole pack of lies. There never was military academy. He had never had an Uncle Oedipus. It was all nonsense, of the sort that these misguided Freudians like to hear. And as for the accusations against Unterholzer – even if Unterholzer had behaved appallingly in criticising his hypothesis, that was no excuse for him, a von Igelfeld, to stoop to that level. He remembered his scorn for Unterholzer when Unterholzer had claimed to be von Unterholzer. Now he, a real von, was behaving just as badly.

He stood stock still for a moment, consumed by misery. Then, his head lowered in shame, he continued his walk home, his mind a turmoil. Should he rush back and apologise to Dr Hubertoffel? Should he write him a letter and try to explain? Whatever he did, he would look ridiculous.

He paused. His route had taken him past a small Catholic church, set back from the street. And there on the notice board was a sign which read: *Sinned? Confessions are heard in this House of God from 6 pm to 8 pm each Wednesday and Saturday evening. Inside, there is one who listens.* And today, von Igelfeld recalled, was Wednesday, and it was undoubtedly evening.

The inside of the church was half-lit. A woman was kneeling at the altar rail of a small side-chapel, but apart from her the church seemed deserted. Von Igelfeld went forward hesitantly, glancing at the pictures that hung on one wall. The Virgin herself looked down on him, a smile of compassion on her lips. And there was Saint Francis, his hands extended towards the birds, and another saint whom he did not recognise, a finger raised in silent admonition, as if of von Igelfeld himself.

He spotted the confessional and moved towards it. He was not a Catholic – the von Igelfelds had always been Lutheran – but he was familiar with the procedure. You went in and sat on a small bench and spoke to the priest behind the grille. It did not matter whether you were a member of the Church; the priest was there for all manner and conditions of men – mendacious philologists not excepted.

He moved the curtain aside and slipped into the box. There was indeed a small grille and a sound behind it, a rustling of a cassock perhaps, told him that the priest was in.

'Good evening,' whispered von Igelfeld.

'Hello,' said a disembodied voice from behind the grille. 'How are you this evening?'

'Not very well,' said von Igelfeld. 'In fact, I am feeling very bad about a terrible thing that I have done.'

The priest was silent for a moment, as if digesting the information. Then he spoke: 'Terrible? How terrible, my son? Have you killed a man?'

Von Igelfeld gasped. 'Oh no! Nothing that bad.'

'Well then,' said the priest. 'Most other things can be undone, can't they? Tell me what this terrible thing is.'

Von Igelfeld drew a deep breath. 'I lied,' he said.

'Lied?' said the priest. 'Lied to the police? To your wife?'

'To a psychoanalyst,' said von Igelfeld.

There was a strange sound from behind the grille, a sound which was rather difficult to interpret, but which sounded rather like disapproval.

'That is *very* bad,' said the priest. 'Psychoanalysts are there to help us. If we lie to them, then we are lying to ourselves. It is a terrible thing.'

'I know,' said von Igelfeld. 'I told him all sorts of lies about my past. And I even made up words in the free association.'

'Both of those things are sins,' said the priest firmly. 'Free association is there to help the psychoanalyst unlock the secrets of the mind. If you mislead in that respect, then the analysis is distorted.'

'But worse than that,' went on von Igelfeld. 'I told lies about my colleague, Unterholzer. He had published an attack on my book and I wanted to ruin his analysis.'

'I see,' said the priest. 'And now you are feeling guilty?'

'Yes,' said von Igelfeld.

'Guilt is natural,' said the priest quietly. 'It is a way in which the Super-ego asserts itself in the face of the primitive, anarchic urges of the Id. Guilt acts as a way of establishing psychic balance between the various parts of the personality. But we should not let it consume us.'

'No?' asked von Igelfeld.

'No,' said the priest. 'Guilt fuels neurosis. A

small measure of guilt is healthy – it affirms the intuitive sense of what is right or wrong. But if you become too focused on what you have done wrong, then you can become an obsessive neurotic.'

'I'm sorry,' said von Igelfeld. 'I truly am sorry for what I have done. Please forgive me.'

'Oh, you're absolved,' said the priest. 'That goes almost without saying. God is very forgiving these days. He's moved on. He forgives everything, in fact. What you have to do now is to repair the

damage that you have caused. You must go and see this Unterholzer and say to him that you are sorry that you have lied about him. You must ask his forgiveness. Then you must write to Dr Hubertoffel – I assume that you're talking about him, by the way, and tell him what you told him about the military academy was untrue. I went to a military academy, incidentally.'

'Oh?' said von Igelfeld. 'Were you unhappy there?'

'Terribly,' said the priest. 'We were crammed together in dormitories, sharing everything, and they made us take cold showers all the time. I still shudder when I take a cold shower.'

'You still take them?' asked von Igelfeld.

'Yes,' said the priest. 'I must confess that I do. I suppose that it's ritualistic. But it may also be that it invokes memories of the military academy and I suspect that there's part of me that wants to remember that.'

'You should forget,' said von Igelfeld. 'You should try to move on.'

'Oh, I try,' said the priest. 'But it's not always easy.'

'But if we may return to my case,' said von Igelfeld, hesitantly. 'Am I truly forgiven?'

'Of course,' said the priest. 'In the name of the Father, the Son and the Holy Ghost. Forgiven entirely.'

Von Igelfeld returned home in high spirits. He had taken to this agreeable priest and had decided that he might well return to listen to some of his sermons. They would surely be very entertaining, unlike the Lutheran dirges he recalled from his boyhood. Filled with the spirit of forgiveness, he wrote an immediate letter of apology to Dr Hubertoffel and went out into the street to post it. Then, retiring to bed, he fell into the first sound sleep that he had had since the awful article had first appeared in the *Zeitschrift*.

★ ★ ★

Unterholzer looked at him suspiciously when he went into his office the following morning.

'Good morning, Herr Unterholzer,' von Igelfeld said brightly. 'I have come to apologise.'

Unterholzer gave a start. This was not what he had expected.

'Yes,' von Igelfeld continued. 'I have done you several great wrongs.'

'Several?' stuttered Unterholzer.

Von Igelfeld looked up at the ceiling. He had not expected it to be easy, and indeed it was not.

'There was the matter of your poor sausage dog,' he said. 'That was most regrettable. I can only assure you that I had not intended that to happen.'

'Of course not,' said Unterholzer. 'I never said that. . . .'

Von Igelfeld cut him short. 'And then I went off to Dr Hubertoffel and tried to ruin your analysis. I told him all sorts of lies.'

Unterholzer's jaw dropped. 'You told him lies about me?'

'Yes,' said von Igelfeld. 'I had intended that he should form a bad impression of you and that your analysis should come to an end.'

For a moment Unterholzer stared mutely at von Igelfeld. Then he began to smile. 'But that's very convenient,' he said. 'I've been looking for a way out of all that without offending Dr Hubertoffel. Now he will be pleased if I no longer go. Frankly, I found it all an expensive waste of time. I've already paid him thousands, you know.'

'So you're pleased?' asked von Igelfeld lamely.

'Absolutely,' said Unterholzer, beaming even more. 'He kept trying to make me something I was not. I don't like to be an assertive, gregarious person. That's not my nature.'

'You're right,' said von Igelfeld. 'Well, I must say that I'm glad that I have been able to help you.'

Unterholzer had sunk back in his chair and the smile had disappeared. 'But I have something for which to apologise,' he muttered. 'I wrote a very spiteful piece about *Portuguese Irregular Verbs*. I did it because of my sausage dog, but now I really regret it. Did you see it?'

'No,' said von Igelfeld. *Truth Always*. 'Well, perhaps I glanced at it. But it was nothing.'

'I shall do all that lies in my power to correct it,' said Unterholzer. 'I can assure you of that.'

'You are very kind, Herr Unterholzer,' said von Igelfeld. 'Let us now put all this behind us and get on with the important work of the moment.'

And that is exactly what happened. The life of the Institute returned to normal. In the next issue of the *Zeitschrift* there appeared a prominent piece by Unterholzer, entitled *Further Thoughts on von Igelfeld's Portuguese Irregular Verbs*. It amounted to a complete recantation of the earlier piece, which was described as having been intended only to engender debate, written by one who had cast himself, unwillingly, in the role of *Avocatus Diaboli*.

It was a thoroughly satisfactory outcome. Only

the Librarian had appeared to regret how things had turned out.

'Poor Herr Unterholzer seems to have lost his new drive,' he commented to von Igelfeld. 'I wonder why?'

'No idea,' began von Igelfeld, but then corrected himself. *Truth Always*. 'At least I think I know, but these matters are confidential and I'm very sorry but I simply cannot tell you.'

THE BONES OF FATHER
CHRISTMAS

Italy beckoned, and this was a call which Professor Moritz-Maria von Igelfeld always found very difficult to resist. He felt at home in Italy, especially in Siena, where he had once spent several idyllic months in the Istituto di Filologia Comparata. That was at the very time at which he was putting the finishing touches to his great work, and indeed many of the streets of that noble town were inextricably linked in his mind with insights he experienced during that creative period of his life. It had been walking along the Banco di Sopra, for example, that he had realised why it was that in Brazilian Portuguese there was a persistent desire to replace the imperative tense with the present indicative. Was it not linked with the tendency to confuse *tu* and *voce*, since the singular of the indicative had the same form as the imperative singular *at least for the second person*?

It was: there could be no other explanation. And had he not rushed back to the Istituto, oblivious to the bemused stares of passers-by? Had he not stumbled briefly on the stairs as he mentally composed the paragraph which would encapsulate this insight, a stumble which had caused the prying concierge to whisper to his friend in the newsagent next door, 'That German professor, the tall one, came back from lunch yesterday *drunk*! Yes, I saw it with my own eyes. Fell downstairs, at least two flights, head over heels.'

And then there was the idea which had come to him one morning while he took a walk past the Monte di Paschi bank and had seen the bill-poster slapping a notice on the wall. The poster had been one of those announcements that the Italians like to put on walls; the death of a local baker's mother. *E morta!* the poster had proclaimed in heavy, Bodoni type, and below that, simply, *Mama!* Von Igelfeld had stopped and read the still gluey text. How remarkable that private pain could be so publicly shared, which meant, of course, its dilution. For we are all members of one another, are we not, and the baker's loss was the loss, in a tiny way, of all those fellow citizens who might know him only slightly, but who would have read his cry of sorrow. And like Proust's tiny madeleine cakes dipped into tea, the sight of one of these posters could evoke in von Igelfeld's mind the moment when, after passing on from that melancholy sign, he had suddenly realised how the system of regular vocalic alternations had developed in the verb *poder*.

But Siena was more for him than those heady days of composition; he cherished, too, a great affection for the Sienese hills. He liked to go to the hills in spring, when the air was laden with the scent of wild flowers. His good friend, Professor Roberto Guerini, was always pleased to entertain him on his small wine estate outside Montalcino, where von Igelfeld had become well-known to the proprietors of surrounding estates and was much in demand at dinner parties in the region. One of these dinner parties was still talked about in Italy. That was the occasion when the current proprietor of the neighbouring estate, the Conte Vittorio Fantozzi, known locally as *il Grasso* (the fat one), had conducted a lengthy dinner-table conversation with von Igelfeld in which both participants spoke old Tuscan dialects now almost completely lost to all but a small band of linguistic enthusiasts. In recognition of his guest's skill, the count had bottled a wine which he named after the distinguished visitor. The label showed a picture of a hedgehog in a field, an allusion to the literal translation of von Igelfeld's name (hedgehog-field, in English, *campo del porcospino* in Italian). Thereafter, von Igelfeld was referred to in Sienese society as 'our dear friend from Germany, *il Professore Porcospino*'.

It would have been good to get back to Tuscany – perhaps even to Montalcino itself – but when the call arrived, it was of a rather different nature.

'Florianus and I are going to Rome,' said Ophelia Prinzel when she encountered von Igelfeld in the small park near his house. 'Would you care to accompany us?'

Von Igelfeld remembered with pleasure the trip to Venice which he had made with the Prinzels a few years earlier. It was true that the holiday had been cut short, when Prinzel discovered that he had been rendered slightly radioactive as a result of contact with polluted canal water, but that had soon been dealt with and was not allowed to place too much of a pall over the trip. Von Igelfeld might have been more pleased had the offer been to go to Venice again, or even to Naples or Palermo, but Rome in the agreeable company of his two old friends was still an attractive prospect, and he accepted readily.

'As it happens,' he said, 'I have some work I've been meaning to do in Rome. I shall be able to spend the days in the Vatican Library and then devote the evenings to leisurely pursuits.'

'So wise,' said Ophelia. 'A break is what you need. You push yourself too hard, Moritz-Maria. I'm quite happy to leave the Puccini project for weeks at a stretch.'

Von Igelfeld was not surprised to hear this, and was tempted to say: *That's why you'll never finish it*, but did not. He had grave doubts whether Puccini's correspondence would ever be published, at least in the lifetime of any of them, but loyalty to his friend forbade any comment.

They set off at the end of April, winding their way down to the plains of Lombardy. They had decided to break the journey, spending a few days in Siena before making the final assault on Rome. From their hotel, perched on the top of the city walls, they had a fine view of the surrounding country-side and its warm, red buildings. Von Igelfeld sat on the terrace and gazed out over the terracotta-tiled rooftops down below him, reflecting on how everything in Italy seemed to be so utterly in harmony with its surroundings. Even the modern works of man, buildings which in any other country would be an imposition on the landscape, here in Italy seemed to have a grace and fluidity that moulded them into the natural flow and form of the countryside. And the people too – they occupied their surroundings as if they were meant to be there; unlike Germany, where everybody seemed to be . . . well, they seemed to be so *cross* for some reason or another.

If life were different – if instead of being the author of *Portuguese Irregular Verbs*, with all that this entailed, he were a man of independent means, able to spend his time as he wished, then he could live in Italy, in some renovated Tuscan farmhouse. He would rise late, attend to his vines, and then take a leisurely drive into the nearby village to buy his newspaper and collect his mail. Perhaps he would even get married and his wife keep him company and play Schubert on the piano for him in the evening. That would be heaven indeed, but there was no point in dreaming; he *was* the author of *Portuguese Irregular Verbs*, he had no house in Italy, and such domestic comfort as he enjoyed was at second hand, crumbs from the table of the Prinzels. If only Unterholzer had not stolen – yes, *stolen* – from him the charming dentist, Dr Lisbetta von Brautheim who should, if there were any justice, have married von Igelfeld himself. And now he had even overheard Unterholzer talking about buying a small house in Italy! What use would that be to him, thought von Igelfeld bitterly. How could Unterholzer even begin to understand the subtle pleasures of the Italian landscape? How could Unterholzer begin to savour the scent of thyme in dusty summer air, with that great big nose of his? More of a lump than a nose, really, if one came to think about it. If Unterholzer were ever to contemplate a scene of hills and cypresses, all he would be able to see would be his own nose, and perhaps a blur beyond it. Italy, with all its visual treats, would be utterly wasted on Unterholzer, who would do far better to stay in Germany, where people like that were somehow less conspicuous.

But what could one expect? thought von Igelfeld. What could one really expect? There was nothing that could be done about Unterholzer. He should have been something else altogether. Perhaps the Burgermeister of a small town somewhere in Bavaria. Instead of which he had poked his large, unsuitable nose into philology, where it had no business to be. Really, it was most vexing.

He sighed. It was not easy maintaining one's position as the author of *Portuguese Irregular Verbs*. Not only was there Unterholzer (and all that tiresome business with his dog), but von Igelfeld also had to cope with the distinct unhelpfulness of the Librarian and with the unmitigated philistinism of his publishers. Then there was the awkward attitude of the university authorities, who recently had shown the temerity to ask him to deliver a series of lectures to undergraduate students. This had almost been the last straw for von Igelfeld, who had been obliged to remind them of just who he was. That had caused them to climb down, and the Rector had even sent a personal letter of apology, but von Igelfeld felt that the damage was done. If German professors could be asked to lecture, as if they were mere *instructors*, then the future of German scholarship looked perilous. He had heard that one of his colleagues had even been asked whether he proposed to write another book, when he had already written one some ten years previously! And the alarming thing was that people were taking this lying down and not protesting at the outrageous breach of academic freedom which it unquestionably was. What would Immanuel Kant have made of it? What would have happened if the University of Koenigsberg had asked Kant whether he proposed to write another *Kritik der reinen Vernunft*? Kant would have treated such a question with the contempt it deserved.

It was the old problem of the poets and the legislators. The poets were not legislators, and the legislators were not poets. The wrong people were at the top, in positions where the people at the bottom might do very much better. Look at the sort of people who became Chancellor of Germany! Who were they? Von Igelfeld paused to address his own question. Who were they indeed? He had very little idea, but they were certainly very dull people, who were, on balance, best ignored. Sooner or later they went away, he found.

'Oh dear!' said von Igelfeld, out loud. '*Il nostro mondo! Che tedio!*'

'My goodness,' said a rich, rather plummy voice behind him. 'What a sentiment!'

Von Igelfeld turned sharply. Somebody had addressed him from behind.

'My dear sir,' said the man standing behind him. 'I did not mean to make you start! It's just that I, too, was admiring this view and reflecting on the state of the world, but was reaching an optimistic conclusion when you expressed yourself.'

Von Igelfeld rose to his feet and bowed slightly to the stranger.

'I am von Igelfeld,' he said.

The stranger smiled. 'And I'm the Duke of Johannesburg,' he said warmly, reaching out to shake hands.

Von Igelfeld looked at the Duke. He was a tall man, seemingly in his mid-forties, almost as tall as von Igelfeld himself, but more heavily-built. He had a fine, aquiline nose, rather reddened, von Igelfeld noted, a large moustache, and a crop of dark hair, neatly brushed back in the manner of a 'thirties dancing instructor. He was wearing a lightweight linen suit, but in place of a tie there was a red bandana tied loosely about his neck.

They engaged in light talk about the view from the terrace. The Duke was not staying at the hotel, he explained. He had a house of his own several streets away, but unfortunately it had no terrace. So he sometimes came down to the hotel in the evenings to take an aperitif and look out over the hills.

'So that's why I'm here,' he said simply.

They discussed Siena. The Duke explained that he had been spending several months a year there for some time, pursuing his researches. Then, when von Igelfeld mentioned Professor Guerini, they discovered a mutual acquaintance. The Duke, it transpired, had also known Guerini for years and had visited his estate several times. This information broke the ice further, and by the time that the Duke had finished his martini von Igelfeld had been invited back to join the Duke for dinner.

'Not a large party,' said the Duke. 'Just one or two people who are passing through and, of course, my research assistant.'

Von Igelfeld was delighted to accept. He was pleased to hear about the research assistant, too, as this confirmed that the Duke himself was a serious scholar. All in all, it seemed a most agreeable prospect and, after the Duke had gone, he rushed off to inform the Prinzels that he would not be joining them for dinner in the hotel that night. As it happened, this suited his companions well. Ophelia Prinzel had a slight headache and was proposing to have an early night and the heat had destroyed Prinzel's appetite. It was agreed that they would meet for breakfast and then spend the earlier part of the morning in the Cathedral Library, admiring the illuminated manuscripts before hordes of schoolchildren and parties of chattering Japanese tourists began to flock in. Von Igelfeld found Japanese tourists particularly trying. They were often fascinated by tall Germans, and he found it most disconcerting to be photographed by them. It was sobering to contemplate how many photograph albums in Tokyo or Kyoto contained his image, frozen in time, quite out of context, pored over and pointed out to interested relatives of the travellers. Why should they want to photograph him? Had they not seen a German professor before? It was another vexing thought, and so he put it out of his mind in favour of the contemplation of dinner at the Duke's house and the warm prospect of edifying conversation and a good table. The Duke's nose was a good portent. Its colour at the end suggested that a considerable quantity of fine Chianti had suffused upwards, by some process of osmosis. This implied the existence of a good cellar, and a generous hand. Let the Prinzels call room service and gnaw at some inedible little morsel; finer things were in store for him.

The Duke's house was in a narrow street off the Piazza del Risorgimento. An inconspicuous door led off the street into a courtyard dominated by a small fountain. Stunted fig trees grew in terra-cotta pots against the walls and a large black cat sat on a stone bench, grooming its fur. The cat looked up and stared at von Igelfeld for a moment or two before returning to its task.

The main door of the house, on the other side of the courtyard, was ajar and von Igelfeld found no bell to ring. He entered somewhat cautiously, finding himself in a large, well-lit entrance hall. The floor, of black and white marble, was clearly an architectural reference to the famous striped cathedral tower which dominated the skyline a few winding streets away. On the walls, framed on either side by gilt sconces, were paintings of Tuscan scenes, one of a cypress-crossed hillside, another of a young man in the Renaissance style, a notary perhaps, seated at his desk before an open window. The window framed a hillside on which deer grazed and improbable birds strutted.

A door opened at the other end of the hall and a young woman – of nineteen at the most, little more than a girl – emerged into the hall. It was a moment or two before she saw von Igelfeld, and when she did, she gave a start.

She raised a hand to her mouth as if to stifle a gasp. Then she spoke, in foreign-accented but correct Italian. 'You gave me a fright. I was not expecting to find anybody in here.'

Von Igelfeld made a self-deprecating gesture.

'There was no bell,' he said apologetically. 'I should have rung had I found a bell. I do not like to walk into the houses of other people without giving them notice.'

The girl laughed. 'Johannesburg doesn't mind,' she said. 'All sorts of people walk in here. He's always happy to see them.'

'I am glad,' said von Igelfeld. Then, after a short pause, he introduced himself and explained that he had been invited for dinner.

'Oh,' she said. 'So you are the German professor he met earlier today when he slipped out for his martini. He told me about you. He said you were very . . .'

She broke off suddenly, the hand going to the mouth. Von Igelfeld frowned. Very what? he wondered.

'Anyway,' said the girl, quickly recovering her composure. 'You must be wondering who I am. I am Beatrice. I'm the Duke's research assistant.'

Von Igelfeld had been wondering who she was and he was pleased that the research assistant was so refreshingly attractive. His research assistants had been uniformly plain and he had always envied colleagues who seemed to have assistants who were glamorous and vivacious. Indeed, he had once raised the matter with Prinzel, drawing attention to the strikingly beautiful young Russian recently recruited by Professor Vochsenkuhn. She had turned every head at the last Romance Philology Congress and had been utterly charming in spite of her linguistic limitations. She spoke only Russian, which von Igelfeld thought must have restricted her ability to conduct research in Romance philology, particularly since Professor Vochsenkuhn himself was not known to speak any Russian.

Prinzel had laughed. 'The reason why other

people have attractive research assistants, Moritz-Maria, is because they don't recruit them on academic ability. In fact, academic ability is probably the last criterion for selection.'

Von Igelfeld had found himself at a loss to understand.

'But if they have no academic ability,' he had objected, 'why recruit them as research assistants?'

Again Prinzel had laughed.

'Because research assistants often have talents which go beyond pure research,' he had said. 'That is widely known. They provide . . . *inspiration* for the professors who employ them. Inspiration is very important.'

Von Igelfeld was not convinced. 'I still cannot see the justification,' he had said. But Prinzel had merely shaken his head and changed the subject. Now here, clearly, was one of those attractive young research assistants who provided inspiration. Prinzel was evidently right.

Beatrice gestured towards the door from which she had emerged.

'They're in the salon,' she said. 'We should join them.'

She led von Igelfeld through a corridor and into a large room at the rear of the building. One of the walls was entirely covered with bookshelves; the others were hung with paintings of the sort von Igelfeld had already encountered in the hall. At the far end, standing before the gaping mouth of a high marble fireplace, stood the Duke, glass in hand; in a chair to his left sat a grey-bearded man dressed in the long black cassock of an Orthodox priest.

'My dear Professor von Igelfeld,' said the Duke, putting down his glass and advancing towards his guest. 'You are most welcome to this house.'

Von Igelfeld bowed slightly to the Duke and then turned towards the priest, who had risen to his feet and had extended a ring-encrusted hand. For a moment von Igelfeld was uncertain whether he was expected to kiss one of the rings, but the gesture very quickly made itself apparent as a handshake.

'And this,' said the Duke genially. 'This is my old friend, Angelos Evangelis, Patriarch of Alexandria and All Africa Down as Far as Somalia.'

Von Igelfeld shook hands with the Patriarch, who smiled and inclined his head slightly.

'We are a very small party tonight,' the Duke went on. 'But, in a way, that is always preferable.'

'Very much better,' agreed von Igelfeld. 'I cannot abide large parties.'

'Then you should not come to this house too often,' said Beatrice. 'Johannesburg gives large parties every other night, more or less.'

Von Igelfeld felt a flush of embarrassment. He had been unwise to condemn large parties; it was obvious that somebody like the Duke of Johannesburg would entertain on a splendid scale.

'Of course, I like large parties too,' he said

quickly. 'It's just that I can't abide them when I'm in the mood for a small party. It all depends, you see.'

'Of course,' said the Duke. 'I know in my bones when I get up whether it's going to be a large party day or a small party day.'

As this conversation was unfolding, Beatrice had busied herself in obtaining a drink for von Igelfeld and in filling up the glasses of the Patriarch and the Duke. There was then a brief silence, during which the Patriarch stared at von Igelfeld and the Duke adjusted the blue cravat which he had donned for the evening.

In an attempt to stimulate conversation, von Igelfeld turned to the Patriarch and asked him where he lived.

The Patriarch looked at von Igelfeld with mournful eyes.

'I live in many places,' he said. 'I live here. I live there. It is given to me to move a great deal. At present I am in Rome, but last year I was in Beirut. Where shall I be next year? That is uncertain. Perhaps you can tell me.'

'Well,' said von Igelfeld. 'I'm not sure . . .' He tailed off.

'I must explain that the Patriarch is currently afflicted with schisms,' interjected the Duke. 'He has been so afflicted for some years.'

Von Igelfeld was about to express his sympathy, but Beatrice now intervened.

'The Patriarch is a very brave man,' she said. 'If

I had schisms I would not know where to turn. Is there a cure?'

The Duke took a sip of his wine. He was smiling.

'Dear Beatrice,' he said. 'Your question is so utterly pertinent, but, alas, one thousand years of Coptic history cannot be so easily resolved. I suggest, therefore, that we go to table. Signora Tagliatti has prepared some wild boar for us and my uncorked wines will rapidly lose their impact if we keep them waiting much longer. Shall we go through?'

In the Duke's dining room, von Igelfeld sat flanked by Beatrice and the Patriarch, with the Duke, a beaming host, at the head of the table. The Duke spoke of his researches – an investigation of the concept of empathy in Hume and compassion in Schopenhauer.

'Much the same thing, don't you think?' he asked von Igelfeld.

Von Igelfeld was not sure. He remembered reading that Hume believed that our minds vibrated in sympathy, and that this ability – to vibrate in unison with one another – was the origin of the ethical impulse. And Schopenhauer's moral theory was about feeling, was it not; so perhaps they were one and the same phenomenon. But he could hardly pronounce on the matter with any authority, having not read Schopenhauer since boyhood, and he looked to Beatrice for support.

'Schopenhauer!' she murmured dreamily.

'You must know a lot about him,' encouraged von Igelfeld.

'Hardly,' she said.

Von Igelfeld was silent for a moment. Was it her role, then, merely to *inspire*? He looked at the Patriarch, who stared back at him with melancholy, rheumy eyes.

'I have known many who have lacked compassion,' the Patriarch said suddenly. 'The pretender to the Bishopric of Khartoum, for example. And the Syrian Ordinary at Constantinople.'

'Especially him,' agreed the Duke.

Von Igelfeld was surprised at the bitterness with which the Patriarch spoke – a bitterness which seemed to find a ready echo in the Duke's response.

'Your schisms,' von Igelfeld began. 'They are clearly very deep. But what are they actually *about*?'

'A variety of important matters,' said the Duke. 'For example, there is a serious dispute as to whether a saint's halo goes out when he dies or whether it remains lit up.'

'It does not go out,' said the Patriarch, in the tone of one pronouncing on the self-evident.

'Then there's the question of miracles,' went on the Duke. 'There is a major schism on the issue of miracles. Are they possible? Does God choose to show himself through the miraculous? That sort of schism.'

'But of course miracles exist,' said Beatrice. 'Miracles occur every day. We all know that. You yourself said that it was a miracle when you and I . . .'

The Duke cut her off, rather sharply, von Igelfeld thought.

'Be that as it may,' he said. 'But it is not really the personal miracles that are at issue. It's the miracles of ecclesiastical significance that are the real substance of the debate. The Miracle of the Holy House, for example. Did angels carry the Virgin Mary's house all the way to Italy from the Holy Land, as is claimed?'

'Of course they did,' said the Patriarch. 'No sensible person doubts that.'

The Duke of Johannesburg

Von Igelfeld looked down at his plate. Had five fish appeared on it at that moment, it seemed that nobody would have been in the slightest bit surprised. But, for his part, he had always found the story of the Holy House rather too far-fetched to believe. How would the house have withstood the flight, even in the care of angels? It seemed to him highly improbable.

Over breakfast the next morning, von Igelfeld reflected on the experiences of the evening. He had enjoyed himself at the Duke's dinner party, but had come away moderately perplexed. Who was Beatrice, and why did she know so little about Schopenhauer? Who was the Patriarch, and who was behind the schisms which seemed to cause him such distress? If he were the Patriarch, then could he not unilaterally put an end to schism simply by expelling schismatics? That is what von Igelfeld himself would have done. Unterholzer, after all, was a sort of schismatic, and von Igelfeld had found no difficulty in dealing with him decisively. Presumably patriarchs had at their disposal a variety of ecclesiastical remedies that put fear into the heart of any dissident. Inverted candles – snuffed out; that was the ritual which von Igelfeld associated with such matters and that would surely silence all but the most headstrong of rebels.

And then there was the mystery of the Duke himself. Von Igelfeld did not purport to know anything about the non-German aristocracy –

which he considered to be a pale imitation of its German equivalent – and he had never been aware of a Dukedom of Johannesburg. But the British were peculiar – it was well-known – and they used extraordinary titles. Was there not a Scottish nobleman simply called The MacGregor, as if he were a whisky? And the Irish were not much better, when one came to think about it. There was a man who went under the title of The McGillicuddy of the Reeks, and somebody actually called the Green Knight. The Green Knight was now defunct, he had heard, which was not at all surprising. What were these people thinking of when they assumed these ridiculous names? At least in Germany people used simple territorial designations which let you know exactly where you stood.

The Duke appeared to be a man of substance. The house was in every respect suitable for aristocratic inhabitation, with its rich furnishings and its air of solid age. But there had been one very peculiar experience which had made von Igelfeld wonder whether all was how it seemed. As he was leaving, he had passed too close to one of the paintings in the hall and had tilted it slightly. He had stopped to straighten the heavy gilt frame, and as he had done so his finger had inadvertently come into contact with the canvas. It was a painting of a sixteenth-century papal coronation, presumably by an artist of the time, and von Igelfeld had touched the lower corner, which showed a crowd amassed outside the gates of the Vatican. This was unexceptional, but what was quite astonishing was the fact that the paint had not quite dried! He had been too surprised to investigate further and anyway the Duke of Johannesburg had appeared at this point and it would have been rude to be seen testing the dryness of one's host's oil paintings. Indeed it would be tantamount to a suggestion of *nouvelle arrivisme*.

The German party breakfasted together on the terrace. Ophelia Prinzel had quite recovered from her headache and was looking forward to a day of wandering about Siena. Prinzel himself had acquired an appetite overnight and tucked into three large almond rolls with apparent gusto, washing them down with at least four cups of steaming milky coffee.

'Wonderful!' Prinzel exclaimed at the end of breakfast. 'Now to the Cathedral before the hordes arrive. Then a browse in the antique shops followed by lunch and a long siesta. What a marvellous day lies ahead of us!'

They walked together to the Cathedral, which had just opened its doors for the day. A taciturn attendant admitted them to the Cathedral Library, where the great illuminated manuscripts lay in their glass cases, displaying their medieval delights to the eyes of moderns, most of whom were now as virtually incapable of using a pen as was the *profanum vulgus* of those distant years. Von Igelfeld concentrated on the finer points of medieval Latin grammar as displayed in the text, while Prinzel and Ophelia discussed the use of colour in the elaborately ornamented capitals or on the bestiary upon which the monks based their parables.

'Look,' said Ophelia, pointing at a page of intricately illuminated text. 'A hedgehog. Moritz-Maria, come and look at this hedgehog.'

Von Igelfeld crossed the room. His family crest contained a hedgehog, as one might expect, and he always felt a tug of affection towards hedgehogs in all their manifestations. It was a noble creature, he thought, every bit as impressive as more conventional heraldic creatures, such as the eagle. Germany, it was true, used the eagle as its symbol, but von Igelfeld had often thought that a hedgehog would be more suitable. It was not impossible to imagine the Prussian flag with a hedgehog rampant rather than its severe eagle.

'Dear little hedgehog,' said Ophelia, pointing at the tiny creature monastically caught in a scurry across the bottom of a page of the Psalms. 'Look how timid he is. Minding nobody's business but his own. Compare him with that boastful unicorn.'

'The hedgehog is not timid,' said von Igelfeld sharply. 'In iconography, I must point out, he represents sagacity.'

'No,' said Prinzel. 'That's the owl.'

'Not only the owl, Herr Prinzel,' snapped von Igelfeld. 'The hedgehog has always been admired for its wisdom. You will be familiar, I assume, with what Pliny the Elder thought about hedgehogs? Or what the *Physiologus* says of their virtues?'

'This hedgehog doesn't look very wise,' said Ophelia. 'Perhaps the monk used as his model a hedgehog which happened not to be very bright. Aristotle made the same mistake about moles when he said that all moles were blind. It's just that the mole he examined was blind.'

Prinzel now joined in. 'And then there's St Basil,' he said. 'Did he not say that hedgehogs were unclean?'

Von Igelfeld glared at his friends. He had not come to this holy and learned place to be insulted, and he thought it best to withdraw to the other side of the room and leave the Prinzels to engage in whatever misguided discussion of symbolism they wished. He had found an interesting example of the ablative absolute in the transcription of a psalm and he wished to ponder it further.

It was while he was studying this text that the doors suddenly opened and the attendant wearily admitted a large group of Japanese visitors. There was a collective intake of breath as they saw the painted ceiling. Several dozen cameras were immediately produced and flashes of light followed hard upon one another. Then the leader of the group gave a cry when he noticed von Igelfeld and called out some command in Japanese. This was the signal for a large group, cameras at the ready, to advance upon von Igelfeld.

'Tall sir,' said the leader as he approached. 'Be

so kind as to stand with me in this photograph.'

Without waiting for an answer, the leader positioned himself next to von Igelfeld and looked up at him in admiration.

'You would be a living monument in Japan,' he said politely. 'Japanese people like very tall people and very tall trees.'

Von Igelfeld stood tight-lipped as the photographs were taken. Really, the whole morning was proving to be quite insupportable. Firstly there had been the tactlessness of the Prinzels, and now there was this Japanese imposition. It was all too much, and as soon as the Japanese had departed he announced to the Prinzels that he had decided to leave and that he would meet them at lunch. It transpired that they, too, were beginning to find the library oppressive and would welcome some fresh air. So the German party left and soon found itself seated in a pleasant pavement café, with the soft morning sun warm upon their brows and the flags waving in a balmy breeze. There was no more talk of hedgehogs and von Igelfeld decided that he would overlook the earlier, ill-advised remarks of his friends. One did not come to Italy to argue; one came to Italy to allow the soul to bask in the sheer beauty of art and its ennobling possibilities.

Von Igelfeld enjoyed his siesta that day. It had been an exhausting morning in one way or another, and when they returned to the hotel after lunch he felt disinclined to do anything but sleep. He woke up shortly after four and read for three hours or so before venturing out for a short walk. He was due to meet the Prinzels for dinner at eight, in a restaurant which had been recommended to them by the hotel manager, and he decided to spend the hour until then wandering about the back alleys of the town. This was a time when people were quite lively, preparing for their evening meal, gossiping with one another, performing the final chores of the day.

He was walking up a narrow street – too narrow for cars, but wide enough for the occasional hurtling moped – when he felt a tug at his sleeve. He turned round sharply and saw the Patriarch standing behind him.

'Professor von Igelfeld,' said the priest. 'I hoped that it was you.'

Von Igelfeld greeted him courteously. Was he enjoying the evening? he asked. And how was the Duke? Had he seen him?

'Yes, yes, yes,' said the Patriarch quickly. 'Wonderful evening. The Duke is in good spirits. I saw him this morning.'

Von Igelfeld waited for something more to be said, but the Patriarch merely looked over his shoulder furtively. Then he turned round and tugged at von Igelfeld's sleeve again.

'Could we please talk for a moment?' he asked. 'There is a little courtyard here on the right. It is always deserted.'

Intrigued, von Igelfeld followed as the Patriarch

led him into the dusty, disused courtyard. The Patriarch still seemed anxious and only when they had crossed to the farther side of the courtyard did he begin to talk.

'Professor von Igelfeld,' he began. 'I should like to ask a favour of you. I need your help. Indeed, the whole Church needs your help.'

For a moment, von Igelfeld was at a loss as to what to say. 'But I don't see how I can help the Church . . .'

The Patriarch brushed aside the objection. 'You can help in a way which is small, but which is also big. Small and big.'

The Patriarch had something tucked under his cassock, which he now took out and held before him. Von Igelfeld saw a small, candy-striped box, with a domed-top, the corners of which were lined with brass fittings.

'This reliquary,' said the Patriarch, 'contains relics of the very greatest significance for the Church. Inside this box there rest the bones of St Nicholas of Myra. They are the object of the most particular reverence in the Coptic Church.'

Von Igelfeld looked at the box in astonishment. He knew that St Nicholas, the bishop of Myra in Turkey in the fourth century, was the original model for none other than the Saint Nicholas, or Santa Claus, of popular legend. These, then, were the bones of Father Christmas.

The Patriarch now held the box out towards von Igelfeld.

'I want you to look after these for me,' he said. 'There are schismatics in the Church who would dearly love to seize them and use them to sow dissension. While they are with me, they are in danger. If you take them, I can recover them from you at some time in the future. It will not be long. You said you were going to Rome for a month. I could get them back from you while you are there. By then, the danger will have passed.'

Von Igelfeld felt the box being thrust into his hands. 'But why have you chosen me?' he stuttered. 'We have only met once.'

The Patriarch looked up at him and gave a rare smile. 'I can tell that you are a man of integrity. I can entrust these to you in the confident expectation that you will not let me down.'

Von Igelfeld looked at the box again.

'You may open it, if you wish,' said the Patriarch. 'But please don't lose the bones. Without them, my Church is bereft and my own position is considerably weakened.'

'I shall do my best,' said von Igelfeld.

'Thank you,' said the Patriarch. 'Now I must tell you where I shall be in Rome and you tell me where you shall be. But please do not attempt to contact me. Nor, if you come across me in public, must you appear to recognise me. *Rome has ten thousand eyes* and there are many there who would wish to weaken our cause.' He paused, fixing von Igelfeld with that disconcerting, mournful stare. 'Do I have your agreement?'

It seemed to von Igelfeld as if there was no alternative. There was an air of such sadness about the Patriarch that it would have been churlish to decline to help him. And besides, it was a small thing to look after a reliquary. It could be tucked into his suitcase and left there until reclaimed. That was very little to ask when so much was at stake.

'I shall do my best,' he whispered, unconsciously mimicking the Patriarch's conspiratorial air. 'The bones will be safe with me.'

The Patriarch bowed his head. 'You are a good man, Professor von Igelfeld,' he said. 'May the protection of Saint Nicholas himself be with you now and in the days to come.'

And with that he slipped away, leaving von Igelfeld standing in the tiny, dark courtyard with the holy striped box nestling in his hands and a hammering within his breast. There were still so many questions to be asked, but there would be time enough for that in the future. Von Igelfeld's immediate task was to stride back to the hotel through the streets of Siena, the box tucked under his jacket. If there were schismatics abroad, even in the heart of Siena, then it would be advisable to have the box safely locked up in his hotel room, away from prying eyes.

They left Siena early the following day, following an indirect, winding route down towards Rome. Von Igelfeld had not mentioned the encounter with the Patriarch, nor had he revealed to the Prinzels the contents of the small overnight bag which he had placed on the seat beside him. Prinzel had attempted to load the bag with the rest of the luggage, but von Igelfeld had resisted.

'That would be safer beside me,' he had said.

Prinzel gave his colleague a sideways look. 'Are you carrying a fortune with you?' he had joked. 'Gold bars perhaps?'

Von Igelfeld had ignored the cheap dig. It gave him some pleasure to imagine that he could offer the Prinzels a prize of any amount – thousands and thousands – to guess the contents of his bag and they would never arrive at the truth. It was, quite simply, an unguessable secret.

And when they stopped for lunch, as they did in a small village at the foot of a hill, von Igelfeld took the bag with him from the car and tucked it away carefully under his chair. Seeing him place it there, the waiter had come forward and sought to take it from him.

'Allow me to put this in the cloakroom, signore,' said the waiter. 'It will be quite safe there.'

'No thank you,' said von Igelfeld firmly. 'I would prefer to have it with me.'

'As signore wishes,' said the waiter sulkily, looking suspiciously at the bag. 'I was only trying to help.'

'Thank you,' said von Igelfeld. 'There are important contents in that bag. That is all.'

'Important contents?' said Prinzel. 'What have

you got in there, Herr von Igelfeld? You weren't so protective of it when we left Germany.'

'No,' said Ophelia. 'And I couldn't help but notice how light it was when we left. Now it is quite a bit heavier. You must have acquired something in Siena.'

Von Igelfeld glared at Ophelia. It was none of her business what he put in his bags. Did he ask her what she had in her luggage? It was a very intrusive thing to do and he was surprised that the Prinzels knew no better.

'Well?' said Prinzel, as he looked at the menu. 'Well?'

'There is something of purely personal value,' said von Igelfeld. 'Something I do not wish to discuss.'

'Oh,' said Ophelia. 'I'm sorry. We have been very tactless. It just seems so strange that you should be so protective of that bag and not tell us what is in it. After all, if I had an important bag I should not be so unkind as to make everybody wonder what was in it.'

'No,' said Prinzel. 'She would not. And nor would I. If you came up to me and said: "What's in your bag?" I would give a civil reply. I would not play some ridiculous game of cat and mouse. I would come straight out and tell you.'

Von Igelfeld stared at the menu. He was again being subjected to intolerable pressure, just as he had been in the museum when they had argued about the significance of hedgehogs. It was as if they were setting out to goad him.

He took a deep breath. It was important not to lose one's calm in circumstances of this sort.

'There is a secret in this bag,' he said quietly. 'You would never imagine – not even in your wildest dreams – how important are the contents of my bag. I have given my word that what is in this bag will not be revealed to others. So please allow me to keep to that undertaking.'

'Oh,' said Ophelia. 'So what is in the bag does not belong to you. You must be carrying it for somebody else.'

'Yes,' said von Igelfeld coldly. 'You could say that.'

The waiter, who had been standing behind von Igelfeld's chair during this exchange, now joined in.

'I wonder if it's anything illegal,' he said. 'If it's so secret, it could be contraband. Are you sure that you aren't being used as some sort of courier? For a terrorist group, perhaps? In which case, I would look out if I were you. The Carabinieri are always prowling around, looking in other people's bags. It would be best if you told us what was in it and we could advise you.'

'Yes,' said Prinzel. 'That would be far better.'

Von Igelfeld twisted in his seat to fix the waiter with his most discouraging stare.

'I am surprised that you should think it your business to enquire as to what your guests have in their bags,' he said icily.

The waiter pouted. 'I was only trying to help,'

he said. 'You Germans think you can carry all sorts of bags around in Italy. Well you can't.'

Prinzel now rose to von Igelfeld's defence. 'It's none of your business,' he said abruptly. 'What is in this bag is between our colleague here and ourselves. It does not concern you in the slightest.'

'You brought the subject up,' said the waiter. 'If this tall gentleman gets himself arrested, then don't say that I didn't try to help.'

'Well we don't want your help,' said Prinzel.

'Then in that case who's going to bring you your lunch?' shouted the waiter.

'Clearly not you,' said Prinzel. 'And there are plenty of other restaurants.'

'Not around here,' said the waiter. 'You're going to go hungry.'

'Oh really,' said von Igelfeld. 'This is all a fuss about nothing.'

'Then why won't you tell us what's in your bag?' crowed the waiter. 'Put an end to the dispute.'

There was a silence. All eyes were turned to von Igelfeld, who looked fixedly ahead.

'I suggest we leave,' said Ophelia, after a moment. 'Our lunch is spoiled.'

They rose to their feet and returned to the car. Not a word was said for at least ten minutes as they continued their journey south. Then Ophelia turned to face von Igelfeld in the back seat.

'Did you remember your bag?' she enquired.

Von Igelfeld sat bolt upright.

'Stop!' he cried. 'Please turn round immediately.'

The waiter was expecting them.

'Hah!' he said. 'Did we forget something? Did we forget a little black bag?'

'Please give it to me this very moment,' said von Igelfeld.

The waiter turned to retrieve the bag from behind the reception desk. Smirking, he handed it over to von Igelfeld.

'So it's bones,' he said. 'What a fuss over a few old bones.'

'You looked!' said von Igelfeld. 'You looked in my bag!'

'Well,' said the waiter calmly. 'It was my patriotic duty. If you had been carrying contraband, I should have had to report you to the Carabinieri. I had to satisfy myself that you were not carrying something illegal.'

'You are an extremely insolent man,' said von Igelfeld. 'I am very surprised that anybody comes to this appalling restaurant.'

'Very few do,' said the waiter.

Von Igelfeld stormed out, followed by Prinzel, who had come in to help retrieve the bag.

'Bones,' mused Prinzel, as they made their way to the car. 'Very strange, Herr von Igelfeld. Bones.'

Von Igelfeld sighed. He had no alternative now but to let the Prinzels in on the secret. It was a relief, in a way, as the responsibility for the relics had begun to weigh on him, and he was appalled with his own carelessness in leaving the bag in the restaurant. How could he have faced the Patriarch with the information that he had abandoned his precious charge in a restaurant, where the box was at the mercy of a prying, self-opinionated waiter? Perhaps once the Prinzels knew what was in the bag they would help him guard the reliquary.

The Prinzels listened carefully.

'What an extraordinary story!' said Prinzel, once von Igelfeld had finished his account. 'We shall have to be very careful.'

Ophelia shuddered. 'I feel quite concerned,' she said. 'I can just imagine those schismatics! Moritz-Maria, you are a very brave man!'

Von Igelfeld nodded, acknowledging the compliment.

'We must be vigilant,' he said. '*Rome has ten thousand eyes.*'

The Prinzels said nothing. They were busy digesting this last comment, which made the innocent Italian landscape, normally so benign in its aspect, seem so strangely threatening. Ahead lay Rome, with its great weight of history and intrigue. What had been intended to be an entirely ordinary month of quiet work in the cool depths of the Vatican Library now threatened to be a month of furtive watchfulness. Von Igelfeld was not sure if he relished the prospect, but he had undertaken to perform a duty on behalf of the Coptic Church and he would carry it out to the letter. The bones would be guarded carefully, and it was only when the Patriarch came to claim them that the candy-striped box would be handed over to its owner. That, at least, was the plan.

The Pensione Garibaldi was one of the quietest and most respectable pensions in Rome. It had been established in the nineteen twenties by a retired civil servant who had secured a lucrative contract for the accommodating of other middle-ranking civil servants visiting Rome from the provinces. These were people who could not afford to stay in the hotels de luxe, but who expected a standard of comfort in keeping with their position. After all, if you were the Deputy Head of the customs office in Bari, in Rome for a three-day meeting on preferential tariffs, you would be entitled to expect a reasonable view and your own table in the dining room. You would also expect a desk clerk who would address you properly as *Ragionere* and take any telephone calls without asking for your name to be spelled out letter by letter. The Garibaldi provided all this, and more, and when the civil servants went elsewhere they were easily replaced by German scholars in Rome to avail themselves of the city's libraries and galleries. It was in the Pensione Garibaldi that the art historian, Gustave Hochler, stayed while writing his *Life of Caravaggio*, and it was at the much sought-after table in the window of the pension's small library that Professor Edmond Winterberg penned his devastating critique of

Humperdinck, suggesting that it was Wagner who wrote passages of Humperdinck rather than the other way round!

Prinzel had been the first to discover the Garibaldi and had in due course recommended it to von Igelfeld.

'Rome is so noisy,' he had said. 'It's almost as bad as Naples in that respect. The Garibaldi is a haven of quiet.'

Von Igelfeld had spent two weeks there while visiting *la Sapienza* and had fully endorsed Prinzel's views. Now the three of them were back again, and there was the same man at the desk who greeted them all as if they had never been away. Von Igelfeld was given the room he had occupied last time, and the Prinzels were given a room at the back, overlooking the carefully cultivated garden with its white marble figure of Augustus and its lily-covered pond.

Von Igelfeld lost no time in ensuring that the reliquary was safely stored in his wardrobe. This was a large mahogany cupboard with a sturdy lock, and it was clear that nobody would be able to gain entry to it without the exertion of considerable force. In an establishment like the Garibaldi, with its well-ordered atmosphere, the prospect of that happening was slight.

The bones secured, von Igelfeld went out and took a coffee in the small coffee bar at the end of the street. He felt a strange sense of exhilaration: not only had he a month of stimulating work ahead of him but he could also look forward to enjoyable architectural rambles with his friends the Prinzels. In every respect, it promised to be a most rewarding time. Not even the newspaper, which he read over his coffee, could dampen his mood. It reported that the Government had fallen – which was nothing unusual, thought von Igelfeld – and one of the judges of the Supreme Court of Italy had shot a fellow judge in the course of an argument. Again, there was nothing surprising in that, reflected von Igelfeld. Fortunately the judge had survived and had taken a remarkably tolerant view of his brother justice's action.

'We are all human,' he had said from his hospital bed. '*Nihil humanum mihi alienum est.* The work of the court must go on.'

The following day, while the Prinzels went off to the nearby Villa Borghese Gardens, von Igelfeld made his way to the Vatican Library. He had secured advance permission to work in the Library, which he had used before. He was interested, in particular, in the manuscript sources, including several volumes of bound correspondence from early Jesuit missionaries in Goa. Although they wrote their formal reports to the Vatican in Latin, a number of them had appended notes in Portuguese, and one or two of them had actually commented on the reception of Portuguese terms in the East. This was a topic of considerable interest to von Igelfeld, who had once written a paper on the origin of the word *alfandica*.

An *alfandica* was a customs house for foreign merchants in India, and was obviously derived from the Portuguese *alfandega*. But was this really based on the Arabic, *al-funduk*, which signified an inn? If the Italian term was *fundaco*, this might not be expected to have a Moorish connection, or might it? There were many similar examples.

It was one of von Igelfeld's favourite libraries. The real pleasure of working there lay in the knowledge of the great and beautiful things with which the Library was filled. Here were the very earliest books, the purest texts of the classics, the finest products of Renaissance Humanism. Here was a sheer accumulation of cultural treasures that outshone that of any other library in any other country. And it was all at his fingertips, ready to be brought to him, on his request, by one of the obliging library staff.

Because of his status, von Igelfeld was allowed to use a special reading room beyond the main public section of the library. This was a room with an airy, open aspect, decorated with sixteenth-century frescoes. There were six or seven large tables in this room, each equipped with several book rests on which large volumes could be safely placed. The chairs in this room were commodious, and well-padded – a fact which had somnolent results for some of the more elderly scholars who frequented this part of the Library. One cardinal in particular was known to retreat to the Library for long hours at a stretch, thereby avoiding duties in his office and enjoying, under the pretence of scholarship, an undisturbed siesta.

Von Igelfeld established himself at a table in the middle of the room, spread out his papers, and called for the first volume of letters to be brought to him. This was a volume which he had not examined before, and he found it to contain a substantial amount of dross. But there were one or two letters which would repay closer study, and these he prepared to transcribe.

The first day of work went well. That evening, he had dinner with the Prinzels in a restaurant near the Garibaldi, and then took an evening walk with them through a pleasant neighbouring part of the city. The next day, he was back at the Vatican Library shortly after it opened, and spent a satisfactory day wading through his manuscripts. He dined alone that night – the Prinzels were at a concert – and retired early to bed, his head still full of the whirls and cursives of the Jesuit script which he had spent the day deciphering.

On the third day, uncomfortably hot outside, but cool in the scholarly inner sanctum of the Vatican Library, von Igelfeld's concentration on his task was considerably interrupted by one of the other readers. This reader, who was at the table next to his, had arrived with one or two other people, and had set himself down to browse through a large folio volume which the Prefect of the Library himself, an ascetic-looking Monsignor, had brought and placed on the table before the reader. Then the Prefect had retired, but there had followed a succession of other visitors who had come up to the table to whisper to the reader or to pass him notes.

Von Igelfeld felt his annoyance growing. Any scholar of standing knew that the library rule of silence had to be respected, even at the cost of considerable personal inconvenience. If this person wished to talk to his friends, then he should go out to do so under the Library portico. It was very distracting for everybody else if conversations were carried out in the library, even if they were *sotto voce*. Von Igelfeld gave a loud sigh, hoping that his fellow reader would notice his displeasure, but the offender merely looked briefly in his direction and met his gaze – rather impudently, thought von Igelfeld. Then, a few minutes later, a cleric came in, approached the other table, and proceeded to have a five-minute conversation, neither of them bothering to lower their voices to any extent. This, in von Igelfeld's view, was the last straw and when the cleric had gone he rose to his feet and approached the offending reader at his table.

'Excuse me,' he began. 'Since you came in this morning you've done nothing but chat to your friends and create a general disturbance. I would have you know that there are serious scholars working in this library and we find it very difficult if people like you don't respect the basic rules.'

The reader looked at him in astonishment. It

was obvious to von Igelfeld that he was barefacedly unrepentant. Well! Let him think about what had been said and he would, if necessary, make an official complaint to the Prefect of the Library if matters did not improve.

Turning on his heel, von Igelfeld returned to his seat and took up his work again. He was pleased to see that the Prefect must have noticed what was happening, as he had gone across to the other reader and was having a whispered conversation with him. He was presumably telling him off, thought von Igelfeld. As well he might! He noticed that the reader shook his head briefly – denying it! thought von Igelfeld – and the Prefect went back to his office. A few minutes later, the noisy reader decided that he had finished his researches – some researches thought von Igelfeld – and left the library.

As von Igelfeld was preparing to leave the Library that evening, the Prefect, who had been hovering around all afternoon, beckoned him over to his office.

'Professor von Igelfeld,' he said, his voice lowered. 'I understand you had some difficulty this morning.'

'I did,' said von Igelfeld. 'There was an extremely noisy reader. People kept coming in to see him and he kept talking. It was thoroughly inconsiderate behaviour on his part. So I told him to keep quiet – in no uncertain terms!'

The Prefect shook his head. 'Most unfortunate,' he said. 'Most regrettable.'

'Unfortunate that I told him off?' said von Igelfeld indignantly. 'That sort of person needs to be reminded of Library rules. It was not the slightest bit unfortunate.'

'Well,' said the Prefect quietly. 'That was the Pope.'

For a few minutes von Igelfeld was unable to say anything. He stood there, rocking slightly on the balls of his feet, as he contemplated the enormity of what he had done. He had told the Pope to keep quiet in his own library. It was a solecism of quite monumental proportions; something that, if it were ever to be related, would simply not be believed. There was nothing – *nothing* – with which it could be compared.

He closed his eyes and then reopened them. He was still in the Vatican Library, standing before the Prefect of the Library, who was looking at him reproachfully over his half-moon spectacles.

'I didn't realise,' von Igelfeld began, his voice thin and reedy. 'I had no idea . . .'

'Evidently not,' said the Prefect dryly. 'In past times, that would have been a most serious offence – it probably still is, for all I know. His Holiness is an absolute monarch, you know, and his writ clearly runs to this library.'

Von Igelfeld nodded miserably. He had never before felt so utterly wretched. If an earthquake had struck and swallowed him up it would have been a complete relief. But there was no earthquake, not even a tremor; the walls of the Library continued their same solid witness to his terrible mistake.

'I should like to apologise to His Holiness,' he said weakly. 'Would that be possible?'

The Prefect shrugged his shoulders. 'It's not all that simple to get an audience,' he said. 'There are people who work in this building for years and years and never see him.'

'But could you not ask?' pleaded von Igelfeld. 'On a matter like this – a personal matter – it may be possible.'

With an air of great weariness, the Prefect leaned forward and picked up a telephone. A number was dialled and a brief conversation was had with a thin, tinny voice at the other end.

'You may go tomorrow morning to the Office of Holy Affairs,' said the Prefect. 'There is a Monsignor Albinoni there who will speak to you at ten o'clock. He may be able to help.'

Von Igelfeld thanked the Prefect and made his way out of the Library like a man leaving the scene of his crime. He took a taxi back to the Garibaldi, gazing steadfastly down at the floor of the vehicle rather than look out, as he normally would, on the streets and piazzas.

'Are you all right?' asked the taxi driver solicitously at the end of the journey. 'You seem very sad.'

Von Igelfeld shook his head.

'You are kind to ask,' he said. 'I am all right. Thank you for your concern.'

'Nothing is that terrible,' said the driver quietly. 'Remember, there is no despair so total that it shuts out all the light.'

Von Igelfeld thanked him again for his advice, paid the fare, and made his way into the pension. Ophelia, who was in the entrance hall studying a map, saw him enter and greeted him enthusiastically.

'We found the most wonderful antiquarian book-dealer, Moritz-Maria,' she began. 'All sorts of things . . .' She tailed off, noticing her friend's crestfallen expression.

'Has something happened?' she asked, taking hold of von Igelfeld's arm.

'Yes,' he said. 'I've done something absolutely unforgivable.'

Ophelia gasped. 'You've mislaid the reliquary again?'

'No,' said von Igelfeld. 'Worse than that. I told the Pope to keep quiet in his own Vatican Library.'

Ophelia gasped again. By this time, Prinzel had wandered into the hall and was told by his wife what had happened. Together they led von Igelfeld to a chair and listened while he explained what had happened.

'But you weren't to know,' said Prinzel soothingly. 'Presumably he was sitting there like any other reader. If he does that, then he can't expect not to be mistaken for an ordinary person from time to time.'

'Perhaps,' said von Igelfeld. 'But that makes me feel no better.'

'I'm not surprised,' said Ophelia. 'I can imagine just how you feel.'

The Prinzels did their best to ease von Igelfeld's burden of guilt and embarrassment, but by the time that he set off for his appointment at the Vatican the following morning he felt every bit as bad – possibly worse – than he had felt before. Nor did the atmosphere of the Office of Holy Affairs do anything to help his mood. This was an austere suite of rooms located at the end of a winding corridor; a place without light. Von Igelfeld had been given a small pass to give him access, and the motif at the top of this looked remarkably like a prison portcullis. The Office of Holy Affairs, it would seem, had some sort of disciplinary role.

Monsignor Albinoni was waiting for him. He sat impassively behind his desk while von Igelfeld narrated the circumstances of the previous day's encounter with the Pope and his only indication of a response was a slight intake of breath when von Igelfeld repeated the words he had used in his scolding of the Pope. Then, when von Igelfeld finished, he uttered his response.

'There is no precedent for this,' he pronounced. 'I feel, therefore, that I should refer you to my immediate superior, Cardinal Ponthez de Cuera. I will speak to him immediately.'

The Cardinal, it transpired, would see von Igelfeld without delay. A young priest was summoned and he led an increasingly miserable von Igelfeld out of the Office of Holy Affairs, back down the corridor, and up a rather intimidating set of marble stairs. At the head of the stairs he knocked at a large set of double doors, which were shortly opened to admit von Igelfeld to a large, airy room with a view over St Peter's Square.

The Cardinal was reading a book when von Igelfeld was admitted. He rose to his feet graciously, straightened his scarlet cassock, and shook hands politely with his visitor.

'I am so sorry to disturb you, Your Eminence,' began von Igelfeld in Portuguese. 'I am Professor von Igelfeld from Regensburg.'

The Cardinal beamed. 'Professor Moritz-Maria von Igelfeld, author of *Portuguese Irregular Verbs*? The very same?'

For the first time that day, von Igelfeld felt the cloud of depression that had hung over him lift slightly. He acknowledged his identity and the Cardinal clapped his hands together with satisfaction.

'But I have long admired that book,' he exclaimed. 'My principal academic interest, you see, is the philology of the Romance languages. And there is nobody who understands the history of our dear Portuguese language better than yourself, dear Professor von Igelfeld.'

Von Igelfeld could hardly believe his good fortune. From the role of criminal, he had been transformed into his proper status, that of the author of *Portuguese Irregular Verbs*. The relief was overwhelming.

'And see!' said the Cardinal, pointing to a large, glass-fronted bookcase. 'There is your book. In pride of place.'

Von Igelfeld glanced at the bookshelf and smiled. There indeed was *Portuguese Irregular Verbs*.

'But my dear Professor,' went on the Cardinal. 'What brings you to the Vatican, and to my fortunate door?'

Von Igelfeld described the events of the previous day and the Cardinal listened intently.

'So I should like somehow to apologise to His Holiness,' finished von Igelfeld.

The Cardinal nodded. 'Of course,' he said. 'A very good idea. I'm sure that the Holy Father will not hold it against you. But it would be nice to be able to say sorry in person.' He paused, looking down at his watch. 'Why don't we try to get him now while he has his coffee?'

Von Igelfeld was astonished. 'You mean . . . now. In person? I had not thought of seeing him; I merely wanted to write a note.'

'But I'm sure he would appreciate a visit,' said the Cardinal. 'Look, you wait here while I nip through and check. He's only a few doors down the corridor.'

Von Igelfeld spent a few nervous minutes before the Cardinal returned and announced that the Pope would receive him for coffee.

'I'm afraid it will just have to be the two of you,'

the Cardinal explained. 'I am terribly behind on some correspondence and must get it done. But perhaps you and I could meet for lunch afterwards? We've got a terribly good Italian restaurant downstairs.'

A Swiss Guard escorted von Igelfeld from the Cardinal's office. They walked down a corridor and through another set of high double doors. Now they were in an ante-room of some sort, at the end of which was a further set of double doors surmounted by the keys of St Peter. Two further guards, standing outside these doors, now moved smartly aside to allow von Igelfeld to pass and to enter the room beyond.

The Pope was sitting at a small coffee table, reading a copy of the *Corriere della Sera*. When he saw von Igelfeld enter, he rose to his feet and waved.

'Come over here, Professor von Igelfeld,' he said. 'The coffee is still warm.'

Von Igelfeld moved over to the table and reached out to take the Pope's hand. Then, still holding the papal hand, he bowed slightly.

'Good morning,' said the Pope warmly. 'Good morning, and blessings. Please sit down and I'll pour the coffee.'

Von Igelfeld sat down.

'I've come to say how sorry I am about that regrettable incident yesterday,' he said. 'I had no idea it was Your Holiness.'

The Pope laughed. 'Oh that! Think no more of that. It's good of you to come and apologise. You know, there are so many who expect us to apologise to them. They ask us to apologise for the Inquisition, to apologise for the over-enthusiasms of missionaries of the past, to apologise for all sorts of terrible things that happened a long time ago. And nobody ever comes to apologise to me! Except you. It's really quite refreshing.'

'Well,' said von Igelfeld. 'I am very sorry indeed.'

'No need to say any more,' said the Pope. 'It's very good to have the chance to chat to you. I have a wretchedly boring time for the most part. You've got no idea what a tedious life it is being Pope. I'm totally isolated from the rest of humanity. You saw me yesterday on one of my rare busy days. Do you know how many social invitations I received last year? No? Well, I shall tell you. None. Not one. Nobody dares to invite the Pope to anything. They all assume that I would never be able to come, or that it would be presumptuous to invite me. So I get none. And I sit here most days and play solitaire. That's what I do.'

The Pope pointed to a table at the side of the room and von Igelfeld saw that it was covered with cards in a solitaire pattern.

'Do you play solitaire yourself?' asked the Pope.

'No,' said von Igelfeld. 'I used to. But not any more.'

The Pope nodded, looking slightly despondent.

He took a sip of his coffee and stared out of the window. For a few minutes nothing was said and the only sound in the room was that of ticking from a long-case clock behind the Pope's chair. Then the Pope sighed.

'I look out of my window and see the Vatican gardens,' he said. 'The trees. The greenery. The paths where I take my walks. The fountains. And I remember a field behind my house in my native village. And I remember the river beyond it where we used to swim as boys. We had a rope tied onto the branch of a tree and we used to swing out over the water. And I've never had any greater pleasure since then. Never. And I've never had any better friends than I had then. Never.'

'We all have a land of lost content,' said von Igelfeld. 'I used to go and stay on my grandfather's estate near Graz. I liked that. Then, a bit later, when I was a student, my friend Prinzel and I used to go walking down the river and drink a glass of beer in a riverside inn. That's what we used to do.'

The Pope said nothing. But, after a moment, he spoke in a quiet voice: 'Now I have my solitaire. I suppose that is something.'

The clock chimed. 'Heavens,' said the Pope. 'That's the end of the coffee break. I must get back to my solitaire. Could you possibly show yourself out? The Swiss Guards will direct you.'

The Pope rose to his feet and ushered von Igelfeld to the door.

'Goodbye, dear Professor von Igelfeld,' he said. 'Good bye. We shall not meet again in this life, I fear, but I have enjoyed our brief meeting. Please remember me.'

And with that he turned and went back to his solitaire table, leaving von Igelfeld in the care of the guards.

The Prinzels insisted on being told every detail of von Igelfeld's remarkable day. Ophelia quizzed him closely as to the decoration of the Pope's private apartment and as to the precise exchange of views which had taken place between them. Prinzel was more interested in the geography of the Vatican and in the mechanism of obtaining an audience; it had seemed so easy for von Igelfeld, but surely it could not be that easy for others. Perhaps all one had to do was to insult the Pope first – if one had the chance – and then insist on an audience of apology

But there had been more to von Igelfeld's day. After he had left the Pope's apartment he had returned to the Vatican Library for some time before the Cardinal had come to collect him for lunch. Then they had gone downstairs to a remarkable restaurant, patronised only by clerics and their guests, where a magnificent Roman meal of six courses had been served. He and the Cardinal had got on extremely well, discussing a variety of philological matters, and von Igelfeld had enjoyed himself immensely. But just as the last dish was being cleared from their table and coffee and liqueurs were about to be served, von Igelfeld had seen a familiar figure enter the restaurant. It was the Duke of Johannesburg. The Duke, who was in the company of an elegantly attired monsignor, had not seen him, and von Igelfeld had been able to make a discreet enquiry of his host.

The Cardinal had turned his head discreetly and glanced at the ducal table.

'The cleric,' he said, 'is none other than Monsignor Ernesto Pricolo. He is the head of an office here which deals with relations with our dear misguided Orthodox brethren. Personally, I find his activities to be distasteful.'

Von Igelfeld shivered. 'Distasteful?'

'Yes,' said the Cardinal. 'He involves himself in their schisms. In fact, I believe he is currently attempting to destabilise the Patriarchy of Alexandria.'

'The Patriarch Angelos Evangelis?' asked von Igelfeld. 'A tall Patriarch with a beard?'

'They all look like that,' said the Cardinal. 'I can never tell them apart. But, yes, that's the one. He has terrible schism problems and our friend Pricolo does nothing to help. Personally, I can't see what possible advantage there is for Rome in it all, but there we are. We are, I suppose, a state and we must do all the things that states do.'

Von Igelfeld succeeded in leaving the restaurant without being seen by the Duke of Johannesburg, but he felt that a cloud had come over the day. If the Duke of Johannesburg was on the side of the schismatics, then he must have deceived the Patriarch into thinking he was really a supporter of his. And if that were the case, then the Duke probably knew, or suspected at least, that the Patriarch had given the reliquary to him, and the schismatics would themselves know that. Which meant that even as he and the Prinzels went about their innocent business in Rome, they could be being observed by the scheming schismatics who would, he assumed, stop at little to retrieve the bones of Father Christmas.

The Prinzels listened carefully to von Igelfeld's account of the lunch.

'This is very serious,' said Prinzel at last. 'We shall have to redouble our vigilance.'

'I suggest that we transfer the reliquary to my cupboard,' said Ophelia. 'They may know that Moritz-Maria has the bones, but they might not suspect us. After all, the Duke of Johannesburg never saw you or myself, did he, Florianus?'

It was agreed that the reliquary would be transferred to the Prinzels' room and hidden in a locked suitcase within their locked wardrobe. This was done, and the evening came to a close. Never had von Igelfeld experienced a more dramatic day: he had met the Pope and over lunch he had witnessed high-level ecclesiastical plotting taking place before his very eyes. In a curious way he was beginning to acquire a taste for this. He imagined that the life of a diplomat, or even a schismatic if it came to it, could be almost as fulfilling as life as a professor of Romance philology. Almost, but not quite.

For the next two weeks, von Igelfeld worked every day at the Vatican Library, only taking off the occasional afternoon to spend with the Prinzels in their architectural explorations. They had intended to visit, and annotate, every important Baroque church in Rome, allowing several days for the study of each church. It was a major undertaking, and already their notebooks were bulging with observations.

Von Igelfeld's own work progressed well. He had unearthed several previously unknown manuscripts thanks to the efforts of the Prefect, who had obviously been informed by the Pope that von Igelfeld was to receive special consideration. And indeed the Pope occasionally sent down a messenger with a small present for von Igelfeld, usually an Italian delicacy – *panforte di Siena* or *amarettini di Sarona* to eat with his morning coffee.

Then, one evening after von Igelfeld had returned to the Garibaldi, he had found a telegram awaiting him. He opened it with some foreboding, as one does with any telegram received while away from home, and saw that the message came from the Patriarch. He was, he explained, in a monastery in the Apennines. For various reasons he was unable to come to Rome to collect the relics, and he wondered if von Igelfeld would be kind enough to come to the monastery to deliver them to him. The relics would be safe there, he assured him.

Von Igelfeld showed the telegram to the Prinzels, who immediately consulted their road atlas and found the town from which it had been sent. The telegram had emanated from Camaldoli, a small town in the mountains, some four hours from Rome.

'If we leave after breakfast tomorrow,' said Prinzel, 'we shall arrive by noon. According to our guidebook there is an inn there. We can stay there and complete our mission the following day.'

The plans laid, they booked themselves out of the Garibaldi, on the understanding that should they wish to return after a day or two there would be no difficulty in finding them rooms. In fact, they were all ready to leave Rome. Von Igelfeld had effectively come to the end of his work in the Vatican Library and the Prinzels were running out of Baroque churches. It was time for a change of surroundings.

The journey to Camaldoli took them high into the mountains of Umbria. From a landscape of rolling hills and comfortable villas they ventured onto mountain roads and broad views of valleys and pine forests. Although it was still sunny, the air now had a sharp edge to it and the streams which cascaded boyishly down the hillsides were icy cold. The inn was exactly as one might expect an old-fashioned Apennine inn to be; wood-panelled, with open fire-places in which the evening log fire had been laid. Each room, which was simply furnished, had a view either of the mountain rising above or the valley falling away below on the other side.

The monastery, they were told, was about an hour's walk away. It could not be reached by car, as it was tucked away on the mountainside above the town. It was too late to go there that after-noon, but they were told that unless an unex-pected mist descended the following morning they could easily make the journey up and down before lunch. That night von Igelfeld slept with the reli-quary under his mattress. He did not sleep well. From time to time he awoke to some sound and froze, thinking that there were schematics outside the door. But the switching on of his light dispelled such terrors, and he would eventually drift back into an uneasy sleep.

At breakfast the next day there was another message. The Patriarch had heard of their arrival and had sent a note with a boy who was making his way down the mountainside to collect bread for the monks. In the note, he explained that he would be down in the town the next day and that they should do nothing until then. 'Please do not leave the hotel,' he warned. 'Even at this late stage, there may be dangers.'

They read and re-read the note, each more frightened than could be publicly admitted. It was decided that they would interpret the Patriarch's warning liberally. As long as one of them was in the hotel at any one time, the others should feel free to wander about the small town or go for a slightly longer walk along the river.

Prinzel and Ophelia went for such a walk after breakfast, leaving von Igelfeld in the hotel. He was sitting in the cramped living room, paging through old Italian magazines and listening to the chatter of the kitchen staff, when the new guests arrived. He looked up to see who they were. Germans perhaps? They were. It was Unterholzer and his wife, and, following closely behind them, their unfortunate dog, with its prosthetic wheels.

There was a great deal of mutual surprise.

'I thought you were all in Rome,' said Unterholzer, pumping von Igelfeld's hand enthusiastically. We had no idea we would meet up with you. What a marvellous coincidence!'

'Yes,' said von Igelfeld reluctantly. 'The Prinzels are here too. They have gone for a walk along the river.'

'Wonderful idea,' said Unterholzer. 'We'll just get everything sorted out and then perhaps you could come for a short walk with us.'

They went off to sign the register and to receive their keys. Then, closely followed by the dog, they went up to their bedroom to unpack.

The Prinzels were late coming back but von Igelfeld decided to risk leaving the hotel before they returned. Since he was with the

Unterholzers, he thought, he could hardly be in any danger. So they wandered off along a path that led into the forest, from which, at various points, they would be afforded a fine view of the valley below.

The walk was most enjoyable, and when they returned the Prinzels were already awaiting them. They were extremely surprised to see the Unterholzers but if they felt any dismay they succeeded in hiding it effectively. Then it was time for lunch, and it was at this point that von Igelfeld made the dreadful discovery.

He went into his room to change the collar of his shirt. At first he saw nothing untoward but after a moment his eye fell on an object on the floor beside his bed. For a moment his heart stopped: it was the reliquary – and it was empty.

He fell to his knees with a cry, seizing the box and lifting it up. The mattress had been disturbed and the reliquary had been pulled from underneath it. He examined it closely: there were strange marks on it, marks which looked, to all intents and purposes, as if they were teeth marks! Some creature had come into the room, smelled out the reliquary, and gnawed it.

He rushed to the door and looked out into the corridor. As he did so, there came a bark from the next door room. Unterholzer's sausage dog! Without wasting a moment, von Igelfeld ran to the open door of the Unterholzers' room and looked inside. Frau Professor Dr Unterholzer was standing in the middle of the rug, wagging a finger in admonition at the dog.

'You are a naughty, naughty creature,' she said severely. 'Where did you get those bones? Now you've eaten them you will have no appetite for your lunch!'

Von Igelfeld stood where he was, his heart a cold stone within him. Unterholzer's dog had achieved, in several quick mouthfuls, what an entire faction of schismatics had so singularly failed to do.

They all spent a bleak and sleepless night. Von Igelfeld felt even worse than he had done when he had told the Pope to keep quiet. At least that was something that could be remedied; there was no possible means of sorting out this dreadful situation with the bones. He had no idea what he would say to the Patriarch when he arrived. He would have to tell him the truth, of course, but that would be such an awful blow to him that he could hardly bring himself to do it.

When the Patriarch eventually arrived the next morning, he immediately sensed that something was wrong.

'The schismatics,' he said. 'They have the bones . . .'

Von Igelfeld shook his head. 'It's even worse than that,' he said. 'I'm terribly sorry to have to tell you this, but Professor Unterholzer's sausage dog ate them yesterday.'

The Patriarch stared at von Igelfeld for a moment as if he did not believe what he had heard. Then he emitted a strange cry – a wail which was redolent of centuries of Coptic sorrow and suffering. Ophelia tried to comfort him, but he was inconsolable, his great frame heaving with sobs.

Unterholzer, who had said nothing during the harrowing encounter, suddenly whispered something to his wife, who nodded her assent.

'Your Holiness,' he said, placing a hand on the Patriarch's shoulder. 'I have the solution. You may have my dog.'

The Patriarch stopped sobbing and turned a tear-stained face to Unterholzer.

'I do not wish to punish it,' he said. 'It's a dumb creature. It cannot be held to account.'

'But that was not what I had in mind,' said Unterholzer. 'I was merely reflecting on the fact that if my dog has eaten those old bones, they become part of him, do they not? He must absorb something.'

The Patriarch nodded. 'He absorbs part of Saint Nicholas. He . . .' He stopped. For a moment he frowned, as if wrestling with some abstruse theological point. Then he broke into a rare smile.

'I see what you are suggesting!' he cried. 'This dog can become an object of veneration during his life. Then, when he eventually dies, we can put his bones in a reliquary too as they will be, in a sense, the bones of Saint Nicholas!'

'Indeed,' said Unterholzer. 'I take it that he will be well looked after?'

'Of course,' said the Patriarch. 'And the schismatics will never suspect that this innocent little dog is the custodian of our most holy relic!'

'A brilliant scheme' said von Igelfeld, feeling extremely relieved. 'A highly satisfactory outcome from all angles.'

Unterholzer's sausage dog was handed over at a touching little ceremony the following day. Then, the whole affair settled, the now enlarged German party settled down to a thoroughly enjoyable celebratory dinner with the Patriarch. Von Igelfeld took the opportunity to warn the Patriarch about the Duke of Johannesburg, but it transpired that the Patriarch had known all along.

'I knew which side he was on,' he explained. 'But I never gave him the impression that I knew. He therefore did not know that I knew.'

'But why is he a schismatic?' asked von Igelfeld. 'What drives him?'

116

'A desire to find a point for his life,' said the Patriarch. 'The feeling that he is being useful to somebody, even if only schismatics.'

'And that young research assistant of his, Beatrice?' asked von Igelfeld. 'What about her?'

'She's actually working for my side,' said the Patriarch. 'She files regular reports for us.'

'Oh,' said von Igelfeld, rather lamely.

'But I'm withdrawing her from active service,' said the Patriarch. 'She has done enough.'

'Will she need a job?' asked von Igelfeld. 'Have you anything for her to do.'

'No,' said the Patriarch. 'But I have just this moment fixed her up with a new post. I spoke to your colleague Professor Unterholzer about her and gave him a full description of her talents. He very kindly agreed to take her on with immediate effect.'

Von Igelfeld was silent. *Unterholzer!* How utterly transparent! He began to shake at the thought of the injustice of it, and was still shaking half an hour later when the party had broken up and he found himself lying in bed in his darkened room, gazing out of his window at the moonlit mountainside. Oh, the injustice of it! Why should Unterholzer, who deserved nothing, get everything? It was so, so unfair.

He took a deep breath. He would rise above this, as he had risen above all the other injustices that blighted his life After all, he was Professor Moritz-Maria von Igelfeld, author of *Portuguese*

117

Irregular Verbs, friend of cardinals and popes. That was something to think about.

He stopped. Should he say friend of cardinals and popes when he knew only one of each, or should he say friend of a cardinal and a pope, or even friend of a cardinal and the Pope?

Puzzling on this difficult point, von Igelfeld eventually fell asleep, and dreamed that he was playing solitaire in a remote field, a long time ago, while at the edge of the field the Pope swung out on a rope over a river that ran silently and very fast. And he was happy again, as was the Pope.

THE PERFECT IMPERFECT

It was clear to everybody at morning coffee that something was tickling Professor Moritz-Maria von Igelfeld. Morning coffee at the Institute was normally a relatively uneventful affair: the Librarian might expound for some time on the difficulties of finding sufficiently conscientious nurses to attend to the needs of his aunt; Unterholzer might comment on the doings of the infinitely wearying local politicians in whose affairs he seemed to take such an inordinate interest; and Prinzel would sit and fiddle with the ink reservoir of his pen, which was always giving him trouble. Von Igelfeld had given up pointing out to him the folly of buying French pens when there were German alternatives to be had, but Prinzel refused to listen. Well, thought von Igelfeld, here we have the consequences – pens that never work and which cover his fingers in ink. *We get the pen we deserve in this life*, he said to himself. It was an impressive-sounding adage, and he was quite pleased to have coined it, but then he began to wonder about its meaning. Do we, in fact, get the pen we deserve? His own pen worked well – and that was possibly a matter of desert – but then Unterholzer had a particularly satisfactory pen, which never went wrong, and which had served his father well too. Unterholzer did not *deserve* a good pen – there could be no doubt about that – and so the theory was immediately disproved. On the other hand, perhaps Unterholzer's father had deserved a good pen and Unterholzer was merely enjoying his father's moral capital. That was quite possible; so perhaps the adage was correct after all.

That morning, when von Igelfeld entered the coffee room with a smile on his lips, Prinzel had removed the barrel of his pen and was attempting to insert a straightened paper clip into the reservoir. Unterholzer was snorting over an item in the local paper and pointing indignantly at the photograph of a politician, while the Librarian browsed through a leaflet published by a private nursing company.

'Something amusing?' asked Prinzel, now attempting to work out how to remove the paper clip from the pen's innards.

'Mildly,' said von Igelfeld.

The Librarian looked at him.

'Do tell me,' he said. 'My poor aunt needs cheering up and I find there's so little positive news I can bring from the Institute.'

'I received a very amusing letter,' said von Igelfeld, extracting a folded sheet of paper from his jacket pocket. He paused, watching the effect of his words on his colleagues.

'Well,' said the Librarian. 'Do tell us about it.'

'It's from a shipping company,' von Igelfeld said. 'They run cruises which go from Hamburg to the Aegean, and they have lectures on these cruises. They have invited me to be one of the lecturers.'

'Oh,' said the Librarian. 'And will you go?'

'Of course not,' said von Igelfeld. 'I am a philologist, not an entertainer. It's an outrageous suggestion.'

'Good,' said Unterholzer quickly. 'In that case, may I write to them and offer my services in your place? I would love to go on one of those lecture cruises. So would my wife. The lecturers can take their wives for nothing, I gather. That is, if one has one, of course, which you don't.'

'I'd very readily go too,' interjected Prinzel. 'I can think of nothing more enjoyable. Sitting on the deck, watching the sea go past! Occasionally having to sing for your supper, but not too often! What a wonderful way of spending a few weeks.'

Von Igelfeld was quite taken aback. He had assumed that his colleagues would have shared his disdain for the whole idea, instead of which they seemed anxious to take his place. This was troubling. Perhaps he had been too quick to turn the company down. In fact, he probably had a duty to do it now, as this would be the only way he could prevent Unterholzer from going in his stead and subjecting all those poor passengers to some terribly dull set of lectures on the subjunctive. It would quite ruin their holidays. No, he would have to re-examine his decision.

'On the other hand,' he said quickly. 'It is perhaps our duty to impart knowledge to the public from time to time. Perhaps I have been too selfish; perhaps I should go after all.'

'But you said that you wouldn't,' protested Unterholzer. 'If your heart isn't in it there is no point in your going. It's not fair to the company or to the passengers. I, by contrast, would be very enthusiastic.'

Von Igelfeld ignored this. 'I think I must go after all,' he said firmly, adding: 'It would be a pity to disappoint the organisers. I'm sure that you would do it very well, Herr Unterholzer, but the organisers did ask for me and not for you. If they had wanted to get you, then they would have written to you rather than to me. Perhaps next time, after I have done it, they might ask for you personally. One never knows.'

Unterholzer muttered something and returned to his newspaper. Prinzel, however, was beginning to warm to the theme.

'You know,' he said, 'I've heard about these lecture cruises. They usually get art historians or archaeologists to talk about the places that the ship visits. They have lectures on Minoan civilisation and the like. Or even talks on Byzantine history.'

'My aunt went on a cruise,' said the Librarian. 'They had a famous psychologist who lectured on relationships. My aunt wasn't much interested in that. But they also had a man who told them all about sea trade in the early Mediterranean. She enjoyed that very much, and still talks a lot about it. And I've even heard that they've had Marcel Reich-Ranicki and famous people like that.'

Von Igelfeld beamed. He was pleased to discover that instead of being insulting, the invitation was something of an honour. They must have taken soundings, he thought; they must have asked people for recommendations before they came to me. In fact, it was quite the opposite. The entertainments officer of the cruise company had chosen von Igelfeld's name from a list of German writers on Portugal. Since the cruise was calling in at both Oporto and Lisbon, before steaming on to the Mediterranean, it had been decided that some of the lectures should reflect this fact. They had tried to get the services of an authority on port wine, who was known to give extremely interesting lectures on the history of the trade, but he was being treated in a clinic and could not oblige. So they had picked von Igelfeld more or less at random, noting that he had 'written a well-known book on the Portuguese language'.

'He'll be able to talk about amusing Portuguese folk tales and the like,' said the entertainments officer. 'With a name like that he could hardly be anything but entertaining.'

'I hope so,' said the manager. 'Let's give him a try.'

'And you never know,' speculated the entertainments officer. 'He might be a success.'

The cruise left Hamburg on a warm June evening. It was a large ship, and the voyage was fully subscribed. They would sail down through the English Channel and out into the Bay of Biscay. Their first port of call was Oporto, and after this they would make their way to Lisbon and Gibraltar before entering the Mediterranean. Von Igelfeld's lectures would start after they arrived at Oporto and continue until they docked at Naples. Thereafter, unencumbered by duties, he would be free to enjoy the remaining ten days of the voyage that would take them all the way to Piraeus.

Von Igelfeld had been allocated a cabin on the port side. He was shown the way by a steward, who then left him standing in the doorway,

contemplating his home for the next eighteen days. It was not very large; in fact, it was one of the smaller cabins, and von Igelfeld was very doubtful as to whether the length of the bed would be adequate. And although there was a small table, it was hardly large enough to write upon. Opening a cupboard, he noticed that there were only four coat hangers and a shoe rack with space for two pairs of shoes at the most, and small shoes at that.

For a few minutes he was uncertain what to do. He had only been on a ship once before when, as a research assistant he had accompanied Professor Dr Dr Dr Dieter Vogelsang to Ireland. That was many years ago and he had very little recollection of the accommodation. But the situation was quite different now: far from being the young scholar, happy to make do with what was offered him, he was now Professor Dr Moritz-Maria von Igelfeld, author of *Portuguese Irregular Verbs*. The thought of this spurred him on. If the shipping company thought that they could put the author of *Portuguese Irregular Verbs* in cramped accommodation like this, then they should be promptly disabused of that notion. The thought crossed his mind: *You get the cabin you deserve in this life.* Well, if that were the case he should get something very much larger and more suitable.

Leaving his bags in the corridor, von Igelfeld made his way back to the central reception hall, where the purser and his staff were engaged in the myriad of tasks which accompanied the settling-in of passengers.

'I regret to say, but I think there has been a mistake,' said von Igelfeld, to a smartly dressed officer. 'I need a larger cabin.'

The officer looked him up and down.

'I'm very sorry, sir,' he said. 'The ship is full. We can't really change people around at this stage.'

'In that case, I demand to see the Captain,' said von Igelfeld.

'He's busy,' said the officer. 'The ship is about to leave port.'

'I am busy too,' said von Igelfeld. 'There is a paper which I must complete on this voyage. I must see the Captain.'

A small group of passengers, sensing that something was wrong, had gathered by von Igelfeld's side.

'Why can't he see the Captain?' said one elderly woman. 'Is there something wrong with the Captain?'

'Is the Captain ill?' asked another slightly worried-looking passenger.

The officer sensed that the situation was getting out of control. Ships were breeding-grounds for rumour and, if the passengers got it into their minds that the Captain was ill, or evading them, the whole vessel would be awash with panicky rumours by the following morning.

'Please calm down,' said the officer. 'I shall take you to see the Captain.'

The officer escorted von Igelfeld up a steep flight of stairs and onto the bridge. The Captain, dressed in his formal uniform, was standing over a chart, talking to another officer, while several others were engaged in various tasks. The officer who had escorted von Igelfeld up spoke briefly to the Captain, who glanced in the professor's direction and frowned.

'I really must insist on something more appropriate,' said von Igelfeld. 'If nothing is available, then I must ask you to release me from my obligation to lecture.'

The Captain sighed. If von Igelfeld withdrew, the lecture programme would be thrown into disarray and there would be complaints, which were always troublesome. They only had three lecturers on board as it was, and that was cutting matters somewhat fine.

'Have you nothing else?' he asked the junior officer.

'No, sir. Everything's occupied.'

'Oh, very well,' said the Captain. 'Professor von Igelfeld, you may have my cabin. I'm sure that I shall be comfortable enough in yours.'

Von Igelfeld smiled. 'That's very generous, Herr Kapitan! I had not intended to inconvenience you, but I am sure that this arrangement will work very well. Thank you.'

Before the ship put to sea, von Igelfeld was transferred from his inadequate, cramped cabin to the Captain's gracious quarters behind the observation deck. Not only did he receive a larger sleeping cabin, but he also had a substantial sitting room, with a bureau. This suited von Igelfeld extremely well, and he had soon unpacked his clothes into the copious wardrobe and spread his papers about the bureau. His earlier ill-humour had deserted him and to celebrate the beginning of the voyage he decided to go down to the bar and take a small sherry.

They put to sea in the evening, with the ship sounding its horn and the lights of the pilot boat weaving about in the half-darkness. Von Igelfeld returned to his cabin and spent an hour at work before dinner. In the dining room, he discovered that he had been given a table with several other passengers but a firm complaint to the steward resulted in his being moved to a solitary table near the door. This suited him very much better, and he enjoyed a good meal before retiring to his cabin for the night.

It was three days before they reached Oporto and the first lecture was to be delivered. The company liked to give the passengers a choice, and so at the time that von Igelfeld was to deliver his introductory talk, *Early Portuguese*, one of the other two lecturers, the popular novelist, Hans-Dieter Dietermann, author of a slew of relentlessly contemporary detective novels, was scheduled to deliver his own introductory talk, *The Modern Sleuth*. Von Igelfeld had met Dietermann briefly at a reception given by the

Captain, but had exchanged only a few words with him. He had no idea why the company should engage such a person to lecture to their passengers, and he only assumed that it was to cater for those passengers who found it difficult to concentrate or who would be out of their depth in listening to a real lecture. Poor Dietermann, thought von Igelfeld: a perfectly decent man, no doubt, but not one who should be attempting to lecture to anybody.

The lectures were due to take place at ten o'clock in the morning, while the ship was still five hours out of Oporto. There was an announcement on the ship's public address system as von Igelfeld made his way to the room in which his lecture was to be given. Chairs had been placed in rows, and at the head of the room there was a table with a jug of water and a lectern.

Von Igelfeld walked up to the table and placed his notes on the lectern. Before him, dotted about the room, was his audience of seven passengers. He glanced at his watch. It was five minutes after the advertised time. He was to be introduced by one of the purser's staff, who now glanced at him sympathetically.

'I'm terribly sorry about the turn-out,' whispered the officer. 'Perhaps people are doing something else.'

'Perhaps they are,' said von Igelfeld coldly. 'Perhaps my lecture was not sufficiently well-advertised.'

'But it was!' protested the officer. 'There were posters all over the place. And there was a big notice in the ship's newspaper.'

Von Igelfeld ignored this. 'Let us begin, anyway,' he said. 'There are at least some intellectually curious passengers on this ship.'

The lecture began. After fifteen minutes, two of the passengers seated near the back slipped out. Three of the others, all elderly ladies, now nodded off, while the remaining two, sitting together at the front, took copious notes. After an hour, von Igelfeld stopped, and thanked his audience for their attention. The two passengers at the front laid down their notebooks and applauded enthusiastically. The three who had been sleeping awoke with a start and joined in the applause. Von Igelfeld nodded in the direction of the two in the front and walked out of the room.

On his way back to his cabin, he found the corridors blocked by passengers streaming out of one of the other rooms. Like most of the passengers on the ship, they were almost all middle-aged women, and they all seemed to be in an exceptionally good mood. Pressed against the wall to allow them to pass, von Igelfeld heard snippets of conversation.

'So amusing . . . I haven't read him I confess, but I shall certainly do so now . . . Do you think that the ship's bookshop has his books? . . . Oh they do, I saw a whole pile of them . . . Very interesting . . . I can't wait for his next lecture . . .'

Von Igelfeld strove to catch more, but the comments merged in the general hubbub. One thing was clear, though: this was the crowd on its way from listening to that poor man, Hans-Dieter Dietermann. He must have had an audience of at least three or four hundred, and they all seemed to have enjoyed themselves. How misguided can people be!

He sat alone at his table over lunch, reflecting on the morning's humiliation. He had never before had so small an audience. Even in America, where he had been obliged, through a misunderstanding, to deliver a lecture on sausage dogs, there had been a larger and distinctly more enthusiastic audience. It was obviously the company's fault – possibly the fault of the Captain himself, and there was no doubt in his mind that the Captain should do something about it.

'I am most displeased,' he told the Captain, when he confronted him on the bridge immediately after lunch. 'Not enough has been done to ensure support for my lectures.'

The Captain smiled. 'But I heard that there had been a very large crowd this morning,' he said. 'I understand that it was a great success.'

'That was the other lecturer, Herr Kapitan,' interjected one of the junior officers. 'That was Herr Dietermann.'

Von Igelfeld turned and glared at the junior officer, but refrained from saying anything.

'Oh,' said the Captain. 'I see. Everyone went to the other one and not to yours.'

'Yes,' said von Igelfeld. 'And I would like something done about it.'

'Well, we can't change the programme,' said the Captain. 'That just confuses everybody.' He thought for a moment. 'I could get some of the crew to go. That might swell the audience for the next one.'

Von Igelfeld nodded. 'I am sure that they would find it very interesting.'

The Captain nodded. 'I'm sorry I won't be able to come myself,' he said. 'Somebody has to stay up here. By the way, is my cabin comfortable enough for you?'

'It is quite adequate,' said von Igelfeld. 'I hope that you are comfortable in . . . in that other cabin.'

'I don't notice these things,' said the Captain politely. 'I'm usually so busy I don't get much time to sleep.'

'Most unfortunate,' said von Igelfeld. 'Sleep is very important.'

He left feeling quite mollified by the Captain's sympathetic view of the situation. He had great confidence in the Captain, and indeed at the next lecture, which took place after they had left Oporto, some twenty members of the crew, acting under Captain's orders and all neatly attired in their white uniforms, sat in two solid rows, listening to von Igelfeld's remarks on the development of the gerundive in Portuguese. Their expression, von Igelfeld thought, tended to the somewhat glassy, but they were probably tired, like the Captain.

The next day, von Igelfeld received a visit from the officer who ran the ship's newspaper. She was planning a short interview with all three lecturers, so that she could publish a profile for the passengers to read over their breakfast. She spoke to von Igelfeld about his work and about his interests, noting his replies down in a small notebook. She seemed particularly interested in *Portuguese Irregular Verbs*, and von Igelfeld spent some time explaining the research which lay behind this great work of scholarship. Then she got on to the personal side of his life.

'Now tell me, Herr Professor,' she asked, 'does your wife mind your going off on these lecture cruises?'

'I am unmarried,' said von Igelfeld. 'I was almost married once, but that did not work out.' *Unterholzer*! he thought bitterly. Had Unterholzer not outflanked him in the courtship of Lisbetta von Brautheim then history would have been very different.

'So you would like to get married one day?' she asked.

'Indeed,' said von Igelfeld. 'It is simply a question of finding the right person. You could say, I suppose, that I am ready to propose marriage should the right lady present herself.'

'Ah!' said the journalist. 'You are a professor in search of a wife.'

Von Igelfeld smiled. 'You might say that,' he said. 'However, my heavy workload prevents my being too active in that respect most of the time.'

'But one might have time on a cruise, might one not?' said the journalist playfully.

Von Igelfeld allowed himself a slight laugh. 'One never knows,' he said. 'Life is full of surprises, is it not?'

The profiles of the three lecturers appeared in the ship's newspaper the next morning. There was a fairly long description of Hans-Dieter Dietermann and a summary of his recent novel. He, it was revealed, was married to a Munich kindergarten teacher and they had three young children. The other lecturer was accompanied by his wife, and there was a photograph of the two of them standing at a ship's railing, looking out to sea. Then there was the feature on von Igelfeld, with a word-for word account of the discussion about being single and looking for a wife. Von Igelfeld read this with a certain amount of embarrassment, but he was pleased enough with the lengthy discussion of *Portuguese Irregular Verbs*.

This book, the article said, *is generally regarded as one of the most important books to be published in Germany this century. As a work of scholarship, it is said by many to be without parallel and is known throughout the world. It is clearly a book that we all should read, if we ever had the time. The Company is honoured to have one of the most distinguished scholars in the world lecturing to its passengers – another example of the high standards of excellence which the Hamburg and North Germany Cruise Line has long maintained.*

Von Igelfeld re-read this passage several times. He resolved to drop a note to the officer who wrote it and thank her for her perceptive and accurate remarks. He might send a copy to the Librarian at the Institute – just for record purposes, of course, and Prinzel and Unterholzer would probably like to see it as well, now that one came to think of it.

He arose from his breakfast table, folded the newspaper carefully, and walked out of the dining room. As he did so, some sixty pairs of eyes, all belonging to the middle-aged widows and divorcees who formed the overwhelming bulk of the cruise passengers, followed his progress from the room. These same eyes had just finished reading the profile in the paper, skipping over the paragraph about *Portuguese Irregular Verbs* but dwelling with considerable interest on the passage about von Igelfeld's single status. That was a matter of great significance to them, as it was undoubtedly the case that of the three hundred widows on the ship, at least two hundred and ninety of them harboured a secret wish in her heart that she might meet a future husband on the cruise. Unfortunately, for complex reasons of demography, von Igelfeld *was the only unmarried man on the boat*, apart from the younger members of the crew, who were too young and who were anyway under strict instructions not to socialise with the passengers; and the two hairdressers, who were not suitable, for quite other reasons.

'What a nice, *tall* man,' whispered Frau Krutzner to her friend, Frau Jens. 'Such a distinguished bearing.'

'So scholarly!' said Frau Jens, dreamily. 'And such a waste! I do hope that he meets a suitable lady soon. In fact, I'm sure that I could look after our dear Professor von Igelfeld myself.'

'Frau Jens!' said Frau Krutzner. 'You have many talents, my dear, but I fear realism may not be one of them. Poor Professor von Igelfeld will be looking for somebody a bit younger than you.'

'Such as you?' retorted Frau Jens.

'I was not going to suggest that,' said Frau Krutzner. 'But since you yourself have raised the possibility, well, who can tell?'

There were many similar conversations amongst friends, the general gist of which was to discuss the prospects of snaring von Igelfeld before the voyage was out. Strategies were laid; outfits which had been brought 'just in case' were retrieved from trunks and pressed into service. The two hairdressers, busy at the best of times, were inundated with requests for appointments and there was a serious danger that supplies of hair dye would be exhausted before there was time to replenish stores at Marseilles.

Von Igelfeld himself was quite unaware of all the excitement amongst the passengers. That afternoon, there were due to be two more lectures: *Portuguese: a Deviant Spanish?* from him, and *Romantic Heroes* from Hans-Dieter Dietermann. Von Igelfeld was reconciled to an audience of twenty-five – composed of obedient crew members and the hard core of his own attenders – with the result that he was astonished when he went into the room and found that it was so packed with people as to allow standing room only for late-comers. For a few moments he thought that he had come to the wrong room; that he had wandered, by mistake, into the auditorium in which Hans-Dieter Dietermann was due to speak. But the officer who was accompanying him assured him that they had come to the right place and that the audience was expecting him to lecture.

For the next hour, von Igelfeld lectured to an enraptured audience, composed, with the exception of the crew members, entirely of ladies. Everything that von Igelfeld said, every move and gesture, was followed with rapt attention by the excited ladies, and after the lecture, when von Igelfeld tried to leave, he was mobbed by eager questioners.

'Tell me, Herr Professor,' said one matron. 'Is Portuguese *all* that different from Spanish? I've been dying to know the answer to that question. And my name, by the way, is Frau Libmann. I am from Munich. Do you know Munich well? My late husband had a large printing works there.'

And: 'Dear Professor von Igelfeld! What a marvellous lecture. I hung on every word – every word! I am Frau Baum from Regensburg. Yes, Regensburg too! Do you know Professor Zimmermann? I have known him for many years. Will you perhaps come and have dinner with Professor Zimmermann and myself some day?'

And: 'Herr Professor! I can't wait to read your book! I am trying to read Herr Dietermann's at the moment, but I am sure that your own book is far more interesting. Do they stock it in the ship's book shop, I wonder? Could you perhaps come and help me find it there?'

Von Igelfeld tried valiantly to deal with all these questions, but eventually, after an hour and a half, when it was apparent that the tenacity of his audience knew no bounds, he was rescued by one of the officers and escorted back to his cabin. On the way they passed the bar where, had they looked, they might have seen a disconsolate Hans-Dieter Dietermann sitting on a stool, wondering why it was that his audience had dwindled to eight.

'You were a real hit back there,' said the officer. 'They loved everything you said. It was quite surprising.'

'Oh?' said von Igelfeld. 'Why should it be surprising? Is Romance philology not intrinsically interesting? Why should those agreeable ladies not find it fascinating?'

'Oh, of course, of course,' said the officer quickly. 'It's just that I have never seen so many of our passengers become so . . . how shall I put it? So *intrigued* by one of our lecturers.'

Von Igelfeld bade farewell to the officer and entered the cabin. He felt quite exhausted after the demanding question session and he looked forward to a short siesta before he ventured out onto the deck for a walk. But as he sat down on his easy chair, he noticed that there were several parcels on the table. He rose to his feet and crossed the cabin. He was puzzled: the steward must have delivered something while he was lecturing. But who would be sending him parcels?

There were three. One was a large box of chocolates, to which a card had been attached: *To one who is lonely, from one who knows what loneliness means. Else Martinhaus (Cabin 256)*. The second parcel, which von Igelfeld opened with fumbling, rather alarmed hands, was a handsome edition of Rilke's poems, on the fly leaf of which had been inscribed: *A woman's soul is a huntress, forever in search of him who can quench the soul's fire. To dear Moritz-Maria, from Margarita Jens (second table from yours in the dining room)*. And finally there was a framed picture of the ship, again a purchase from the on-board shop, signed with the following motto: *I will go to the end of the seven seas for you*. The signature on this present, regrettably, was illegible.

Von Igelfeld sat down weakly. This was extraordinary. Why should three ladies whom he had never met take it upon themselves to send him presents? And why, moreover, should they make these protestations of affection when he had done nothing to encourage them to do so? Was this the way that respectable German widows behaved these days? If it was, then Germany had changed utterly and profoundly from the Germany he had once known. It was still necessary, however, to observe the formalities and to thank the donors of the gifts. He would write a note to Frau Jens and ask the steward to deliver it to her table. Frau Martinhaus had given him the number of her cabin and so he could simply slip a note under her door. And as for the donor of the picture, if she could not identify herself properly on her gifts then she should not be surprised to receive no acknowledgment.

Von Igelfeld sat at the Captain's desk and wrote out the notes. He thanked the donors for their kind gifts and expressed his pleasure that they had enjoyed his lecture so much. He trusted that they would enjoy the remaining lectures, and assured them that if he could help them at all – on any point of philology or Portuguese grammar – they had only to ask. The notes written, he had a long, luxuriant bath in the Captain's bath, and then dressed for dinner.

In the dining room, there was a murmur of excitement as von Igelfeld made his entry. This was the signal for five determined ladies, including Frau Jens and Frau Martinhaus, to rise to their feet simultaneously, all with the thought of intercepting von Igelfeld before he reached his table and inviting him to dine at theirs. Victory went to the fastest of these. Frau Jens's legs, unfortunately, were too short to carry her across the room with sufficient despatch, and the first person to reach von Igelfeld's side was Frau Magda Holtmann, the widow of a Bonn lawyer, whose previous skills as a member, some forty years ago, of the University of Gottingen's Women's Sprint Team gave her a distinct advantage over the other four.

Von Igelfeld had no wish to have dinner with anybody, but felt unable to turn down the invitation. So, under glares of barely concealed anger from other tables, the ladies of Frau Holtmann's table enjoyed his company over dinner, each of them thinking privately what a perfect match he would make for them individually and wondering whether fourteen days would be enough to accomplish the task of securing an offer of marriage. Each had gone over the advantages which she might have over her rivals – and rivals there undoubtedly were. In many cases it was fortune – perhaps the Professor had had enough of working in his Institute and would appreciate the life of a private scholar? In some cases it was social prowess – a small, but appreciative salon, perhaps, for the society of Wiesbaden? And in other cases, it was skill in culinary matters. How did a mere man *survive* without somebody to ensure that the table was always properly furnished with good German delicacies? Did the poor Herr Professor eat in restaurants all the time? Did he even get *enough to eat*? Men needed their food – it was well-known. He was very thin; marriage would change all that.

By the end of dinner, von Igelfeld was exhausted. He had spent the entire meal dealing with the ladies' questions. What were his hobbies? Did he have relatives in Munster, by any chance? There had been a Professor Igelfold there, had there not, and the Igelfolds could be a branch of the same family, could they not? Did he enjoy walking? The hills above Freiburg were very suitable for that purpose! Was he ever in Freiburg? Did he know the von Kersell family? There had been a Professor von Kersell once, but something had happened to him. Did he know, by any chance, what that was?

After coffee had been served, von Igelfeld had looked very publicly at his watch and had excused himself.

'I always have to do an hour or so's reading before I go to bed,' he announced. 'And this sea air makes me so sleepy.'

The ladies had nodded their agreement. It was very important, they felt, to get a good night's sleep when at sea, and, indeed, on land as well.

Von Igelfeld rose to his feet, thanked his hostess, and made his way out of the dining room. Frau

Jens, who had been waiting for her moment, reached the door just as he did.

'Why, Herr Professor!' she said. 'It's you!'

Von Igelfeld nodded weakly.

'I was just going for a stroll on the deck,' said Frau Jens. 'It would be a great pleasure if you were able to accompany me.'

Without waiting for an answer, she took him by the arm and led him away. Within the dining room there were sharp intakes of breath at several tables.

'Did you see that!' hissed Frau Martinhaus. 'That shameless woman!'

'Desperation knows no bounds,' agreed her table companion. '*Inter arma silent leges.*'

'Auf Englisch könnte Mann sagen: *Fat arms, tiny legs,*' said Frau Martinhaus, somewhat less than charitably.

Von Igelfeld walked round the deck with Frau Jens for five minutes. Then, wresting his arm from her grip, he excused himself and rushed back to his cabin. There were several ladies in the corridor, and these stopped him briefly, under the pretext of finding out details of tomorrow's lecture.

'We shall all be there!' said one of them brightly. 'Notebooks at the ready!'

Again, it took von Igelfeld several minutes to extricate himself, but eventually he succeeded in reaching the sanctuary of his cabin. Once inside, he locked the door firmly and collapsed into his chair. The day had been a nightmare from start to finish, and he wondered how he could possibly last out for two further weeks. It was all that journalist's fault. If she had not asked him about marriage, then all these ladies would not have had the idea placed in their heads that he was a suitable candidate for them. Perhaps he could ask her to publish a correction: to say that there had been a misunderstanding, and that he actually was married? The problems with that scheme were that she would presumably refuse – as it would make her look foolish – and that it was inherently very improbable that anybody could make so fundamental a mistake. There seemed to be no way out of it: he would have to brave it out for the remaining two weeks, taking as many meals as possible in his cabin and remaining locked up there for as much of the day as was consistent with remaining sane.

The next day, as it transpired, was even worse. Von Igelfeld was pestered from breakfast onwards, constantly being approached by ladies claiming to have an interest in Romance philology. When he retreated to his cabin there was no peace. Either the telephone rang, with an invitation from one of the ladies to join a bridge four or play table tennis, or there was a knock on the door from a caller with the same sort of invitation. The lecture, of course, was now even better attended, and the ladies attempted to outdo one another in donning their finest outfits and more extravagant jewellery.

Hans-Dieter Dietermann's audience had now gone down to three, and the third lecturer, who was giving a short series of talks on the history of Gibraltar had nobody at all to listen to him.

After a further two days, they reached Naples. Von Igelfeld, who had now completed his lectures, received numerous offers to have dinner ashore, but politely turned them all down. The ship stood offshore, rather than docking, and the passengers were conveyed to land in large launches hired for the occasion. Von Igelfeld's launch was dangerously overloaded, as most of the ladies tried to secure a place on it once they knew he was on board, with the result that it almost overturned on the way in. For von Igelfeld, this was the final straw. When he got ashore, he rushed off, leaving the ladies, and hailed a taxi. This he instructed to take him to the railway station. Then, paying off the taxi driver, he gave him a substantial tip on the understanding that the driver would return to the harbour and leave word with the launch office to the effect that he had been called away on urgent business and was not returning on board for the rest of the cruise. It being Naples, however, where research has revealed that sixty eight per cent of the population is profoundly dishonest, the taxi driver merely pocketed the money and did not perform this commission. But von Igelfeld was not to know this; he merely purchased a single ticket to Siena, via Rome, and boarded the next available train. He did not care about his possessions on board ship. These could be sent on to him when the ship returned to Hamburg. He had simply had enough: the whole venture had been misconceived from start to finish.

The ship left Naples early the following morning. Von Igelfeld's absence was noticed at eleven o'clock, when they were five hours out to sea. Enquiries were made and the Captain concluded that the most likely explanation was that he had gone ashore in Naples and simply not returned. This was investigated, and it was at this point that the disturbing information surfaced that the launch tallies added up. Three hundred and eighteen people had gone ashore in Naples and three hundred and eighteen appeared to have returned. This was a miscount, in fact; only three hundred and seventeen had returned, but in these circumstances the Captain was obliged to reach a more sinister conclusion.

Man overboard procedures were begun. The ship stopped in its tracks and a thorough search was made of the entire vessel. There were announcements made on the public address system and the shocked passengers were asked if anybody had seen Professor von Igelfeld that morning. Unfortunately at this point another fatal error was made. Two elderly sisters, of failing eyesight, went to report that they had seen him on the deck that morning at eight o'clock. He had been leaning over the rails, they said, and they were, moreover, sure that it was him. They had been at all his lectures and they knew exactly who he was. They had, in fact, been looking at one of the stewards, who was not yet in uniform, and who was looking out for flying fish at the time.

The Captain ordered the ship about and a slow, melancholy search was made of the portion of sea which the ship had been traversing at roughly eight thirty that morning. Alas, nothing was found, and by the time light faded that evening the grim conclusion was reached that Professor von Igelfeld had been lost at sea. A signal was sent to the company in Hamburg and early the next morning a telephone call was made to the Institute of Romance Philology in Regensburg informing them of the tragedy.

Von Igelfeld had reached Siena on the same day as his sudden departure from the ship and had spent the evening in his usual hotel there. The next morning he had contacted his friend, Professor Roberto Guerini, who had immediately invited him to spend some time on his wine estate near Montalcino. This suited von Igelfeld very well, and the next few days there were many enjoyable walks through the woods and evenings spent in the company of his Italian friends. There was even a dinner party at the house of the Conte Vittorio Fantozzi, which was, as such occasions inevitably were, a noted success.

After the pleasant interlude in Montalcino, it was time to return home. Von Igelfeld, who had been provided by Guerini with clothing and a small suitcase, packed his bag and bade farewell to his friends. Then, thoroughly rested by the break, he caught an express train from Siena to Munich. When he arrived in Regensburg, he decided to go straight from the railway station to the Institute to deal with his mail. Then he would go home and answer the letters that had no doubt built up there in his absence.

Not having seen the German press while he was in Italy, he had of course failed to read the item which was carried by most of the nationals: GERMAN PROFESSOR LOST AT SEA! Nor had he read the fulsome tribute from Prinzel, quoted at length in the same newspapers, or the remarks of other members of the philological community, including Unterholzer, who had referred in most generous terms to *Portuguese Irregular Verbs* and had commented that it was a very great loss indeed that there would now be no successor volume. Even had he read these, he might not have expected to find, on his return to the Institute, that things had been changed, and that a new name had appeared on his door.

'Why are you in my room?' he asked, as he opened the door of his office, to find Unterholzer sitting at his desk.

Unterholzer looked up, and turned quite white. It was as if he had seen a ghost.

'But you're dead!' he blurted out after a few moments.

'I most certainly am not!' said von Igelfeld.

'Are you sure?' stammered Unterholzer. 'Don't be so ridiculous, Herr Unterholzer,' said von Igelfeld. 'There are very few things of which we can be sure in this life, but that, I should have thought, is one of them.'

'I see,' said Unterholzer, lamely. 'The only reason why I am here in this office is that the papers said that you had been lost at sea. I thought that you would like the thought of my having your office after you've gone.'

Von Igelfeld bristled. 'Whatever gave you that idea?' he said sharply. 'I might well have quite different ideas.'

Unterholzer had risen to his feet. 'Oh, Moritz-Maria, I am so pleased that you are alive! I cannot tell you how sad I was . . .' He stopped as he realized his terrible solecism. He had addressed von Igelfeld by his first name, and they had only known one another for, what was it, fifteen years?'

'I'm so sorry,' he rapidly continued. 'I didn't mean to call you that. It was the emotion of the occasion . . .'

Von Igelfeld raised a hand to stop him. He was touched that Unterholzer, for all his faults, had been so upset at his death. One might even overlook his presumption in taking his room, or almost . . .

'Don't apologise,' he said, adding, 'Detlev.'

It was a terrible effort for von Igelfeld to utter Unterholzer's first name, but it had to be done.

'Yes, Detlev, we have known one another for many years now, and it might be appropriate to move to first name terms. So it will be *du* from now on.'

Unterholzer looked immensely relieved. 'Let us go down to the café and drink . . .'

'And drink a toast to *Bruderschaft*,' said von Igelfeld kindly. It was good to be alive, he thought. Life was so precious, so unexpected in its developments, and so very rich in possibilities.

They left the Institute and walked down to the café.

'To *Bruderschaft!*' said Unterholzer, raising his glass. 'To brotherhood.'

'To *Brüderschaft!*' said von Igelfeld.

They sipped at the wine. Outside in the streets, a passing band of students suddenly raised their voices in song, singing those wonderful haunting words of the *Gaudeamus*:

Gaudeamus igitur,
Juvenes dum sumus.
Post iucundum iuventutem
Post molestam senectutem
Nos habebit humus,
*Nos habebit humus!**

* Let us rejoice therefore / While we are young. / After a pleasant youth / After a troublesome old age / The earth will have us.

150

Von Igelfeld smiled at Unterholzer. '*Aut nos habebit mare!*'* he joked. And Unterholzer, who had not heard so good a joke for many years, laughed and laughed.

* Or the sea will have us!